18 HOLES

18 HOLES

A ROUND OF GOLF STORIES

PAUL PAXTON

Copyright © 2023 Paul Paxton

The moral right of the author has been asserted.

Apart from any fair dealing for the purposes of research or private study, or criticism or review, as permitted under the Copyright, Designs and Patents Act 1988, this publication may only be reproduced, stored or transmitted, in any form or by any means, with the prior permission in writing of the publishers, or in the case of reprographic reproduction in accordance with the terms of licences issued by the Copyright Licensing Agency. Enquiries concerning reproduction outside those terms should be sent to the publishers.

This is a work of fiction. Names, characters, businesses, places, events and incidents are either the products of the author's imagination or used in a fictitious manner. Any resemblance to actual persons, living or dead, or actual events is purely coincidental.

Matador
Unit E2 Airfield Business Park,
Harrison Road, Market Harborough,
Leicestershire. LE16 7UL
Tel: 0116 2792299
Email: books@troubador.co.uk
Web: www.troubador.co.uk/matador
Twitter: @matadorbooks

ISBN 978 1803136 981

British Library Cataloguing in Publication Data.
A catalogue record for this book is available from the British Library.

Printed and bound in Great Britain by CMP UK
Typeset in 11pt Minion Pro by Troubador Publishing Ltd, Leicester, UK

Matador is an imprint of Troubador Publishing Ltd

In loving memory of Fred,
whose golf stories were plentiful but never short.

CONTENTS

1st Hole: The Holy Grail	1
2nd Hole: All The President's Men	5
3rd Hole: Swan Song	14
4th Hole: Every Dog Has Its Day	21
5th Hole: For Whom the Bell Tolls	25
6th Hole: Oxshott Golf club	29
7th Hole: One Chance Only	35
8th Hole: The Hayward Cup	39
9th Hole: Mindfulness	43
10th Hole: Wheel Power	45
11th Hole: A Very Modern Game	50
12th Hole: For the Love of the game	54
13th Hole: The Shank	58
14th Hole: Yippie	63
15th Hole: Q School	67
16th Hole: A Long Shot	75
17th Hole: Cash is King	80
18th Hole: Win Some, Lose Some	87

1ˢᵀ HOLE
THE HOLY GRAIL

Samuel Bradley sat in his back office and listened to the excitement next door as his team celebrated. A cheer went up as an additional bottle of Moet Champagne was popped open. He put down his plastic cup half filled with champagne, picked up the data sheet, and put his feet up on the desk. The evidence was clear cut; the key independently assessed data for accuracy, distance, spin and robustness, had exceeded expectations – they had done it! The quest to produce a GPS-tracked golf ball, one that actually worked, had broken the hearts and pockets of many before them. Even on their own project, 'Operation Holy Grail,' which had lasted two years, there had been more than one occasion when Samuel, the sole director of Sports Engineering Ltd, had considered abandoning the task or been nearly forced to do so by his sceptical bankers.

The challenges were numerous: The primary problem was an essential ingredient: producing a GPS transmitter that was small enough to fit inside the ball without distorting its flight, and one that was accurate to within a metre. Previous technology, developed for sailors in distress, worked well at sea where a life boat or rescue helicopter could easily locate a yachtsman bobbing in the high seas; provided that the GPS reading was within ten metres. Anyone who has hunted for a wayward slice in the long rough on the 5th at Wentworth, or their local municipal course for that matter, will attest that knowing that your ball is *within 10 metres* is just frustrating, not helpful. Samuel and his team had, for ages, not been able to narrow the range down to the initial objective of a metre, but the introduction of an audible bleep from the ball had been a transformation.

It was always assumed that, outside of the technological issues, golf's regulatory authority would be the biggest hurdle to overcome. This assumption was critical because what was the point of producing a golf ball that could not be used in competition? Of greater importance, from a marketing perspective, was that ball sales would be much enhanced by having some of the game's leading players utilising the technology. Samuel had fantasised about watching Tiger or Jordan Spieth strolling casually into the rough to recover their ball; one which the official ball spotters had struggled to find – priceless. In Britain, the rules of golf are set and governed by the famous *Royal and Ancient*, based at St Andrew's Golf Club. They had been surprisingly receptive, given their reputation for stuffiness. Sports Engineering's application had come at a time when the game was desperate to improve playing speeds; slow play had become a curse of the game. This desperation was especially so in the amateur game, where everyone seemed to ignore the new, shorter time limits for looking for a lost ball.

Cost, as ever, was important; producing a £100 golf ball was a vanity project, not a commercial venture. Samuel was so financially exposed now that failure meant bankruptcy and his ball needed to be competitively priced. A recent trip to China had produced the breakthrough required. The Beijing Authorities were trying to bring greater control over the millions of bikes congesting the streets with many simply being abandoned. A bike hire system looked to be the solution. Their enthusiasm for Samuel's GPS technology meant potential increased volume production and as a result, a golf ball *for life* at an affordable price. Even Samuel accepted that the *"Ball for Life"* slogan overstated matters, but putting aside the one off cost of the wrist receiver, the ball at £10 a pop, would transform the game.

Samuel reached for his champagne. It was time to join the celebrations. As he did so, the phone rang and out of habit, he answered.

"Samuel Bradley."

"Hi, Samuel," came the distinctly American voice. "It's Bill Steinbeck, vice president of Golf Enterprises." Samuel knew that Golf Enterprises was the largest manufacturer and supplier of golf equipment in both Europe and the States.

"Samuel, I'll cut to the chase: rumour of your new golf ball has spread – is it true?" There was no need for Samuel to be anything less than candid as he already had patents pending worldwide, albeit he was amazed at the leak of this confidential data that the team themselves had only received an hour earlier.

"Yes, Bill, it's true. At last, an unlosable golf ball."

"We want to buy it. I have instructions to make you a very generous offer."

The call continued for another ten minutes. As Samuel joined the team, yet another cork popped. He knew now that he was financially secure for life. The sum offered represented but a drop in the ocean when compared with the value of Golf Enterprises' worldwide sale of balls. Samuel knew that his invention, the one worked so hard on by his loyal team, would never reach production stage. It would be buried in the Golf Enterprise's archives, along with the other start-up operations that had threatened their profitability.

He wouldn't tell the team just yet…

2ᴺᴰ HOLE
ALL THE PRESIDENT'S MEN

Every United States President since Eisenhower has played golf. It is difficult to say who the best player was, because given the extensive security team that accompanies the leader of the free world, no President has lost a golf ball in over twenty five years. Even wayward balls flying into the Florida Glades reappeared miraculously bank side and with a decent lie. Each of the assigned secret service agents carries with them a couple of balls marked with the unique "Force 1" on them in order to speed up the game and not use up too much of their principal's valuable time; pin positions when the President played were always generous too.

The current president was a golf fanatic. This passion for the game, according to the leader of the terrorist cell, was a vulnerability. One that he intended to exploit. The presidential visit to Dublin had been advertised several months in advance. From a golfing perspective, it was inevitable that the president would want to play the Dublin County Club;

only ten miles outside of the city centre and home of the Ryder Cup's last visit to Ireland. Valuable information.

The idea of laying a trap utilising widely publicised information was, in terrorist circles, nothing new. The IRA bombing of Brighton's Grand Hotel at the Conservative Party Conference was perhaps the best example: a date and venue known a year in advance with public access in the intervening period.

The four-man cell had a plan, but they lacked one valuable ingredient; none of them played golf. The game in their homeland was considered a pastime of the decadent West. There was only one thing to do: they would have to take golf lessons. First, they would want to look the part. Following an internet review, they had individually visited the Golf Superstore where sales for the day must have been at record levels. Ping Clubs, White Hot putters, Pringle jumpers and Titleist Pro Vs balls all found their way into the shopping trolley. One of the plotters had to return: not having realised that he would need left handed clubs, and that his Nike trainers would not fit the bill.

Now for the lessons. They had less than ten weeks to learn to play to a sufficient level that would then enable them to acquire a handicap of at least 18 or less, as the Dublin County Club would not entertain visitors hacking their precious course up. There was therefore a minimum level of competence to meet. An official handicap certificate would, the Club's web site said, "need to be presented upon arrival". They would base themselves in the UK before flying into Dublin. In order to avoid any suspicion, each would join a separate golf club and sign up with the resident pro for lessons. They could then meet up down the golf range in the evening for further practice and refinement of the plan. What their terrorist quarter master made of their expenditure is unclear. He was far more used to expenditure on arms, explosives and bribery, not electric golf trolleys and 19th hole club sandwiches.

The four men were, in effect, full time golfers and the progress they made and their commitment to the game impressed their respective coaches, who had not witnessed such advancement from complete beginners before. In order to attain the essential handicap certificates, it was necessary to submit three competition cards to their club secretary. Much to the irritation of the others, Cell Member 2 even won the monthly Stableford competition, drawing unnecessary attention to his presence. The ensuing invitation to join the men's team for an away match in Surrey the following week was declined was reluctantly declined.

It was now only two weeks before the president's arrival. The visit to Ireland would only be for three days and there was no official indication that the president would even play golf, let alone where and when. However, the terrorists emailed and rang the Dublin Country Club under pseudonyms seeking to obtain a four ball tee time. By doing so, they were able to ascertain that no tee times were available for three days before the president's arrival in the city and the first available slot was on the day of his departure. They were sure of it: the president was coming. His vulnerability confirmed it was time for reconnaissance.

With ten days remaining, the unlikely four ball were greeted warmly in the pro shop by resident pro and raconteur, Jimmy Costello.

"Gentlemen, welcome to the Dublin Country Club. Four

ball for 10.18 – time enough for a hearty Irish breakfast perhaps?" Each of the cell members looked dapper, dressed in their sky blues, yellows and reds. They held their handicap certificate in hand. "Don't worry about those – I can see that you know what you're doing. As long as you keep the trolleys out of the bunkers and don't use your wedge on the greens." The pro laughed heartily at the prospect, whilst the cell members looked at each other wondering if all that time down the golf range had been necessary after all.

The reconnaissance was focussed on finding the green, which afforded the most privacy; one which enabled them to fulfil their bomb making preparations without detection. The 6th was a possibility, but another golfer hunting a lost ball on the adjoining fairway might spot them. They agreed to rule out the par 3s as being too visible and although they were feeling tense, all four managed a smile at the prospect of their plan being ruined by a presidential hole in one.

At last, the perfect set up: the dog leg, par 5, 17th with its isolated green overlooked by nothing but dense woodland. Photographs were taken and the possible pin placements on this tricky sloping green were noted. Today's was towards the front edge; anything short or slightly left would find itself rolling at speed down the bank leaving a nasty chip back. The second hole plug was at the rear of the green but protected by two mounds, each burrowing in opposite directions—treacherous, but there in the heart of the green was the third plugged hole that would surely be the one used for the presidential visit. It was ideal as it allowed for a degree of inaccuracy on entry and the basin that surrounded it encouraged the ball onto the flat area that would reward a straight putt from inwards of 8 feet: the 17th it would be.

As far as they could tell, following a further series of requests to the club, the terror cell had secured the last tee off time before the course was closed. The pro had even warned that with fading daylight, they may not be able to complete the round. *As long as we get to play 17 holes…*

Following the traditional warm welcome and confirmation that they were the last round of the day, the four ball set out on their second round at this prestigious course. Given the dipping sun, it was clear that by the time they reached the 17th hole they would have the course to themselves, for the only golfers they met were making their way towards the clubhouse playing out the final few holes of their round. The men were keen to get to the 17th a soon as possible, but again did not want to draw attention and cutting across fairways would surely do so. When it was clear that they were indeed alone, they headed straight from the 10th green to the 17 tee; they were unseen. Their tee shots on this dog leg, par five were rather good given the circumstance, but as soon as they were around the corner they picked up their balls and marched on to the green.

The pin was at the back of the green this time. Cell Member 1 reached into the adapted side pocket of his Ping golf bag and pulled out two cup cutters. The first was a conventional one used by green keepers the world over— a round thin twin bladed metal tube 4.25 inches in diameter on the end of a T-shaped metal pole.

The tube was turned via the T grip and the blades will cut easily into a well-watered green. The second had been modified in the work shop so that it could cut much deeper, creating valuable space below the cup itself. Member 1 walked to the centre of the green where the easiest pin setting had been identified from the earlier round. He deftly removed the turf plug with a few turns of the handle. Then, he walked back to today's hole. Removing the flag, he knelt down and, using a small pair of pliers, extracted the four-inch deep white aluminium cup from the hole. Deploying the green cutter once again, he robustly inserted the recently extracted tuft into the empty hole. It fitted well but required a firm press from the flat press which, along with the cutters, had also been bought on Amazon. He returned to the freshly cut hole, laid out a plastic sheet to collect any loose soil and inserted the modified cutters, pressing down hard whilst turning the blades. He needed to create a pocket at least eight inches deeper than the bottom of the cup holder itself. He measured the overall depth, using a spoon to extract the final half inch of soil. He was pleased with his work and the practice undertaken at his home course at twilight last week had reaped the rewards. The terrorist had even felt a pang of guilt at having left that 12th green so vandalised, given that his early attempts at hole creation were less skilled than his current efforts. Such damage was worth it for the bigger cause, and he would not be returning to witness his fellow members' anger.

Now, for the dangerous part. The other men kept watch as Cell Member 3, the bomb maker in the team, carefully, though without fear or hesitation, removed the devise from his golf bag. The bomb itself was not particularly sophisticated, but it had the three essential components: explosive, a detonator and a timer. The explosive needed to be a high grade, because there was a limited amount of space in the hole itself. Secondly, in order to ensure the success of the operation, the explosion had to impact all who were standing on or immediately alongside the green at the time of the explosion.

The bomb maker loaded the Semtex into the hole and gently pressed it into position. He then inspected, for the final time, the three-part detonator. The top section was a regular cup, identical to the ones used by the Club. The bottom piece contained the detonator wires that would activate the plastic explosives. The middle section was by far the most innovative: once inserted into the hole, it would simply look like the bottom of the cup, the very cup in which the President or his playing partner's ball would roll. It allowed the insertion of the flag pin without triggering detonation, too. However, given that the terrorists could have no way of knowing when their Presidential target would actually be on the green, an electronic timer was of no use. No one outside of the President's entourage would be allowed anywhere near the course, so there would be no option to observe either. The solution: a sensitive trigger; one that would be activated by the weight of the golf ball as it dropped into the hole. The cup was pushed into position, ensuring that the detonators were secure and that the top of the cup sat just below the top surface of the green itself. Delicately, the bomb maker painted a white circle around the rim to create a professional finish; the greenkeeper would have been proud of his work. The bomb maker looked up at his compatriots; they nodded in acknowledgement for they knew what was to follow. He pulled the small pliers from his pocket and inserted them into the hole. Gripping the bottom of the cup holder, he lifted it until he heard the familiar click. The trigger had been set. They left the flag on the fringe of the green nearest to the clubhouse, knowing then that it would simply be picked up by ground staff who wouldn't notice the change of hole.

The men had no intention of finishing the round, duly making their way back to club house before leaving the club without indulging at the 19th hole. As was Cell protocol, they made their way to Dublin airport where they were booked on a flight to Paris that evening. The trap had been set, and therefore their work had been done.

Four days later the Club Secretary could hardly contain his excitement as he announced to a select group of members gathered around the first tee:

"Ladies and gentleman, first up on the tee, the President of the United States of America."

His resulting drive impressed the gallery. His playing partner today was a business acquaintance with commercial interests on both sides of the Atlantic; his drive also received polite applause from the carefully selected and vetted club members. The two golfers would be evenly matched. The President doffed his cap as he took up his position in the buggy and left the group behind as he headed down the fairway.

At the turn, the men had been all square but having struggled in the bunker at the 11th and having missed a short putt on the 16th, they headed to the 17th with the President two holes down with two to play. The businessman hit his third shot fat and his ball just about made the short rough on fringe of the green. The president on the other hand, hit an impressive enough 7 iron that made the most of the green's contours leaving his ball 4 feet from the death trap. The businessman decided against using his putter and stabbed at the ball with his wedge, catching it thin. The ball raced toward the hole and struck the base of the flag pole. It so nearly dropped. The significance of the chip could have been so much more than a guaranteed half.

"I'll tap it in to get out of your way, Mr. President." The businessman widened his stance so as not to stand on his playing partner's line and nonchalantly prepared to tap the ball in from two feet.

"Take it away, take it away," came the call from the President and rather than hole out, his playing partner knocked his ball towards the waiting buggy. He lifted the flag as the President had requested and withdrew to the side of the green to watch the President line up his putt for the hole. The president twitched a little and shuffled, the short miss at the 16th still in his mind. It was only then that the businessman realised the significance of the putt. If he missed it, the President would have lost the match – the President didn't like losing.

"Mr. President, that sir, in these parts, is a gimme."

"About time too," said the President with a wry smile, relieved not to have to make the putt. He duly picked up his ball. They both headed off to the 18th with both the match and the President still alive.

3ᴿᴰ HOLE
SWAN SONG

Eduardo Lopez had first caddied at the age of ten. His eldest brother, Jarvier, who caddied on a regular basis at the local hotel golf course, had fallen ill and the family couldn't afford to lose out on the 10 peso fixed payment. His father was too infirm to help, and so it was that Eduardo that stepped in to carry a bag nearly as big as himself for what seemed more like four days than four hours. He had certainly learnt his first lesson on the value of money. The American golfer who was holidaying at the 5 star Mexican resort had been sympathetic and patient; he even paid a two peso tip and gave him a can of Coke and a chocolate bar at the half way house.

Eduardo began to caddie on a regular basis in his middle teens. He was a popular choice, for not only was he articulate and polite but he had the ability to find a ball not matter how deep the rough and he read the greens very well. Given that most players were playing the course for the first time as part of their holiday package, his knowledge was of real value to them and he was tipped accordingly. They suspected on occasions that he was not actually finding their ball but dropping one of the same make, but he smiled and so did they. He knew for sure that a winning golfer was more generous than a loser.

The difference between Eduardo and the other pool of caddies was that he actually enjoyed the game. He might even sneak back on to the course at twilight to hit a few putts with an old, broken putter he had picked up from the golf club rubbish bins and repaired. On these occasions, he would also hunt for some spare balls; balls that he could put to good use in later rounds.

Mark Macauley Junior, a wealthy businessman on holiday from California, had insisted in being allocated the club's best Caddie.

"That's an easy one, Mr Macauley; it's Eduardo Lopez, albeit he charges a premium," added the caddie master who also saw an opportunity for a margin.

"They tell me you're good, Lopez. You better be as this is a big money game – do you understand, kid?" This information was passed on to Eduardo without malice or aggression, and Mr Macauley had winked and patted him hard on the shoulder to reinforce the message. The game was match play and the position between the rivals ebbed and flowed, though there was never more than a hole between them. How Eduardo had found the hooked drive in the rough on the 17th remained a mystery to all bar Eduardo himself. His spare supply of Pro Vs had helped. He even carried with him red, blue and black marker pens so that the appropriate markings could be added for those golfers who wanted to ensure they were playing the correct ball. Mark Macauley halved the 17th hole and had a spring in his step as he headed on to the 18th tee all square. He winked again at Eduardo as he returned his putter. Perhaps he knew too.

The standard of golf on the 18th was relatively poor for two players off single figure handicaps. The pressure was telling and Eduardo wondered just how much was at stake. As is so often the case, everything boiled down to the putting green. Both men left themselves difficult second putts; at least eight feet and on a fast green. Macauley's opponent putted first and didn't really commit to the putt, but had left a tap in which was duly conceded. Macauley's putt then, for the match. Eduardo knew the green and this pin position well; he had seen many a miss from exactly his playing partner's position.

"It looks straight as a dye to me, Lopez," Macauley whispered, as Eduardo joined him behind the ball.

"I agree, it looks straight, but I'm telling you it will break a whole cup diameter from right to left. Trust me, senor." Macauley said nothing but crouched again and looked for a break with incredulity.

"You sure, kid?"

"Role it up on the right and watch the baby move…"

Mark Macauley Jr. settled behind the ball and took aim as instructed. Even his opponent let out a sigh of relieve as he saw the ball start out off line for what he also concurred was a straight putt. As predicted, the ball defied the laws of physics and at the last dived into the centre of the cup. Match won – it was time for Eduardo to wink this time. The players shook hands and headed back to the adjoining club house. As they did so, Mr. Macauley pushed a $500 dollar bill into Eduardo's hand.

"Thanks, kid, you deserve it; now if you ever find your way to the Country Club in Sacramento, I've a job for you."
They both smiled.

Poverty and gang culture went hand in hand; violence was never too far away in Eduardo's home town and the contrast in wealth between the exclusive hotels and the adjoining neighbourhoods was stark. Life was cheap. Eduardo resented the extortion money that even he had to pay on his small income, and there was no way he was handing over his $500, let alone the saved money he hid in a tin inside his bed mattress. He didn't know how they knew about the tip that he had received that day, but the other caddie may have seen the hand over. Either way, the gang wanted it; it was time to leave.

The escape across the Mexican border into the United States had not been without risk, but it was a journey that many of his compatriots had made before him. He was now an illegal immigrant in the land of the free. His journey up to the Sacramento Country Club had taken several days; needless to say, security had refused him entry and threatened him with the police. He couldn't read or write, so he couldn't leave a note for Mark Macauley Jr. announcing his arrival. He asked for the security patrolman to pass on a message for him and handed over a Pro V golf ball complete with Mr. Macauley's favoured two red dot marking.

"Tell him this is from Eduardo Lopez," he said handing over the ball to a bewildered security officer. Eduardo also had written his pay-as-you-go phone number on the ball.

Over a week passed before the call came.

"Hey, Lopez, find any lost balls lately?"

Macauley admired Eduardo's guts and innovation. He became his caddie for the next three years. Cash in hand, travel and accommodation expenses if he was playing out of state; always with a win bonus. Macauley liked to play head-to-head money matches, but given his status in the commercial sector he also received plenty of pro-am invitations and accepted a few.

But, it was at his home course, at the Sacramento County Club Pro- Am when it happened: disaster struck for Eduardo.

Mark Macauley Jr. had been a lifelong fan of country music legend Mimi Charliotti. She had just finished yet another successful world tour and at the age of 73 still looked magnificent.

Macauley had seen a photo of her playing golf and she had apparently taken up the game whilst on a recent visit to the UK. Her handicap of 45 was, however, still fully merited. Not without significant expense, Macauley had persuaded her to play in the Pro – Am, following several calls to her agent. It had been less difficult to ensure that she was drawn to play with him. He allowed her to have Eduardo as her caddie, given her propensity to find the rough and the tricky greens.

On the 16th green, Mimi's ball had ended up in the worst possible position. Right on the top of a steep slope. It was a 20-foot putt, which if misread for pace could easily lead to the ball rolling off the other side of the green into the waiting lake. If misread for break, which was a monstrous right to left at nearly 90 degrees the ball would definitely be in the drink. Eduardo had witnessed it on many an occasion. Macauley was sensitive to his super star's pride. The following gallery had enjoyed her banter, but even she had winced at some of her shots albeit she still hadn't lost a ball. That said, Eduardo was down to his last substitute sphere.

"You need to give her a big hand here, Lopez!" called Macauley. Eduardo joined her with the putter at the top of the slope.

"Miss Mimi, it's as fast as hell and you need to aim here," he said, pointing to a spot away from the direction of the hole.

She lined up the putt.

"Sorry, ma'am, not there but here," encouraged Eduardo.

"Why, my cute little Eduardo, let's just do it together!" and to the joy of the gallery, she positioned her caddie behind her and got him to wrap his arms around her small frame. Eduardo, though rather nervous at first, snuggled into the celebrity's bottom and laid his hands over hers, redirecting the angle of the putter in the process.

She yielded to his touch and he pulled the putter smoothly away from the ball and then barely touched it, starting the ball rolling slowly. The gathered audience began to laugh as the ball appeared to come to halt on the brow of the slope less than three feet from where Eduardo and Mimi watched. Eduardo knew though what was to follow and sure enough, almost imperceptibly at first, gravity took hold and the ball started to pick up speed, at the same time traversing the mound. How the crowd cheered as, with the final roll of the ball, it tiptoed into the side of the cup. Eduardo and Mimi hugged and the cameras clicked.

The putt went viral on social media within the hour and the local news featured it on the tea time news. By the evening, it was featuring on both national and international television stations, including MexVisual, the main Mexican news Channel. Though the initial focus of the viewers was on the singer, attention soon turned to the caddie: Edwardo Lopez. The very Eduardo who hadn't been seen since the stabbing to death of two leading gang members in a homestead just outside of Cancun. The gang had found him. Revenge would be sweet, and Eduardo Lopez would be dead within the week.

4ᵀᴴ HOLE
EVERY DOG HAS ITS DAY

Daniel Herman was having the round of his life. He had been a member at Heathcote Golf Club in Hampshire for more than twenty years, yet had never even won the monthly medal. Today, on Club Championship day, he was on fire. Chipping in at the 2nd and 7th had helped and his confidence and had been buoyed by a cheeky up and down from the deep bunker at the back of the 12th.

He had for a short period a few years back got his handicap down to 16.4, but by the time his 60th birthday came around he was comfortable enough off 20 and still couldn't get into the late 30 points at the monthly Stableford, let alone win the medal. But today, he was running away with it and knew it. Every dog has its day, and this was his.

Stroke play off a 3/4 handicap normally played into the hands of a higher single figures handicapper, a good player with a solid game under pressure but with room for a bit of slippage. Joe McGuire, a delightful young member playing off 8, had posted a net 68, two under par, earlier in the day; historically, enough to win the championship. Subject to disaster, and bear in mind when you're playing off 20 that's, by definition, never too far away, Daniel Herman's name would find its way in gold leaf on to the winners' board; a board listing all winners since the clubs inception in 1932.

No need for the driver off the 17th nor the 18th, just punch a rescue club and keep in bounds; a sound strategy any day of the week.

The 18th involved a long uphill walk from tee to green, with the last 100 metres testing the legs of young and old alike. Daniel had gone quiet and said nothing for the last five minutes. His playing partners, who all knew him well, said nothing either, believing that he needed to focus on achieving his moment of glory – wow he had played well.

Daniel began to sweat; was this really how the pros felt as they closed in on a major? His chest tightened and he as good as jerked his wedge, catching it thin but sending it on its way. When your luck is in, you should ride it, and his ball as good as weaved between the green side bunkers. Daniel took a deep breath; he needed it. His surroundings were a bit of a blur now. Two putts and then he'd unwind with a cool pint of lager and a celebratory cigar. He lagged his putt up short, within gimme range for the Sunday four ball, but on Club Championship day everything needed to be holed out.

Daniel took one step forward and then collapsed to the ground; he couldn't speak, but was holding his chest and breathing in gasps. Daniel's brow was dripping with sweat. His playing partners didn't need a medical qualification to know that he was having a heart attack.

Ironically, Daniel had been on the fundraising committee for the club's defibrillator CPR machines, following the death of his good friend, who had collapsed and in the club car park and was dead by the time the paramedics arrived. The first of the fully automatic machines were situated on the 10th hole, which offered decent access from a number of the surrounding holes. The second, which was already on its way to the 18th green, was kept in the club bar and had helped save the life of a member within two weeks of its arrival.

A flick of the 'on' button and the clearest and calmest of voices emitted instructions; by now Daniel's eyes were closed and there was no sign of a pulse. Daniel's shirt was lifted up and the two pads were positioned on his chest.

"Stand back everyone, here we go," called the bar steward who had also administered the last, successful, electric impulse.

The machine counted down: three, two, one.

Daniel's body jolted. Brian, the steward, paused to assess pulse and breathing. Nothing.

"And again…"

Three, two, one.

Same jolt, same result.

"One final try."

Three, two, one.

The surge of electricity brought an immediate response this time. Daniel's eyes opened and his chest started to rise and fall. The steward placed a golf towel under Daniel's head and offered reassurance.

"Daniel, help is on its way. You are going to be fine."

Daniel acknowledged the message with a nod of his head.

He looked next towards the hole and his ball resting two feet from glory.

"No Daniel, no! Lie still."

But Daniel would have none of it. He slowly clambered to his feet and pointed towards his putter. Brian helpfully picked it up for him and to everyone's amazement, he took four steps towards his ball. He was unsteady over it, but wasted no time in hitting it straight into the centre of the hole.

They tried to catch him as he fell again. Neither man nor machine was going to save Daniel this time, but he had died as the club champion.

5TH HOLE
FOR WHOM THE BELL TOLLS

If such records were kept, it would show that more holes in one are scored on the 17th hole of the Mullon on Sea Golf Course than any other course in the country. With its spectacular views over the North Sea and Great Yarmouth in the distance, the course is very popular with holiday makers looking to combine strolls on the sandy *Golden Mile* with a more strenuous challenge on this undulating course. Visitors can hire clubs and even golf shoes as the club sought to encourage trade in the summer months.

The par 3, 17th hole, was only 100 metres to the centre of the green and an accentuated bowl encouraged balls to roll towards the central pin-setting, no matter which side of the green the ball lands. The number of aces was staggering: during the month of August last year there were on average three holes in one per day. Yes, three!

The 17th green was significantly uphill from the tee and the pin is hidden from those playing from below. Inherently, that should make the achievement more difficult; nothing of the sort at Mullon on Sea.

The annual members had always resented the summer influx of players, even if they recognised that their green fees supplemented the running costs of the club. That attitude changed a few years ago when, on the first weekend of the summer holidays, there were two holes in one. Both golfers were thrilled with their achievement and in the time honoured fashion, didn't hesitate to buy all of the members in the club house a drink; the ale was quickly swapped for double whiskeys.

The next day exactly the same thing happened – two holes in one and more free drinks. Suspicions were, of cause, raised and it did not require the services of Sherlock Holmes to discover that Finley Lawton, the teenage son of the club's bar manager had been seeking to entertain himself during the early days of the school holidays by delighting and deceiving the visitors. At an opportune moment, Finley would scramble on to the green and pop the ball nearest to the hole into the cup. From his hiding place, he then enjoyed watching the elation as the golfers excitedly shouted, hugged and shook hands, and then took the obligatory mobile phone photo. The green itself was close to the cliff edge, but otherwise had a barren surround. For that reason, the golfers didn't have to slightest concern that the ace was a genuine one, as they could see that there could be no external influence. Had they bothered to walk to the cliff edge and looked over, they may have spotted Finley crouching in a cove, one better suited for sea gulls than humans.

Whilst Finley had, at first, contemplated putting a ball from every four ball into the hole, he knew that this would quickly put an end to his jolly jape and after all, it was only the start of the summer holidays. Finley's father, Nick Lawton, mockingly castigated his son when he confessed to the pranks but the members toasted him and laughed at his harmless, if rather naughty, behaviour. Not golf etiquette, but where was the harm? The golfers returned from their holiday with a tale to tell and the members enjoyed the flow of large single malts.

And so it was that the hole in one ritual occurred most days in the summer. When Finley was more constructively engaged, he would arrange for a pal, George Henry, to step into his shoes or his cove, to be more precise.

The bar at the golf club was full now most days in August. Finley's father was happy to serve them all, even if a decent percentage of the elderly customers had never played a round in their lives. Word of the scam had spread to the neighbouring village and this had swelled their numbers. Nick had even bought an old brass marine bell for the bar and rang it with relish when the gleeful golfers arrived to announce their good fortune. Not all the 'acers' were keen to buy the celebratory drinks, especially as the numbers increased, but how could someone resist the ringing bell and applauding members?

Large Whiskeys all round it is then, barman.

It was the 22rd of August and Finley was down on his haunches, out of sight at the back of the green. He had already discreetly seen, having watching the group putt out on the adjoining hole, that this was a three ball. He was instantly pleased as the first shot landed on the front of the green and rolled towards the pin. *I'll be able to use that one,* he thought, *they will know it's close to the hole.*

To Finley's surprise, the ball continued on its journey and just like that, it plopped into the hole. Finley felt like cheering himself and almost stood up to call down to the tee. It was the first real hole in one he'd actually seen.

He thought that he should turn back to his hiding place but as he started to head back towards the cliff edge, he was startled as the second ball clattered into the pin; he turned to look but couldn't see the ball.

Had it rebounded into the bunker? Can't see it – surely not...no way.

Crawling on all fours he shuffled towards the hole – peering into it he could see both balls!

Ouch! Cried Finley as the third ball hit him on the back, fell to the ground and rolled the further twelve inches into the hole as well. The win treble.

Finley panicked, no one would ever believe what had happened; or worse, if they did believe it, there would be publicity of the wrong kind for him.

Reaching into the hole he removed all three balls and rolled them across the green in different directions. Finley headed back to his hiding hole.

No ringing bell; no whiskey.

6ᵀᴴ HOLE
OXSHOTT GOLF CLUB

The dispute with our neighbour over his ever growing leylandii trees was affecting my wife's health. Helen and I had politely requested that the trees be cut back or at least stunted, but our request was met with contempt and a shrug of the shoulders.

"It's my garden and I'll do what I like with it."

This was no council estate either; we had paid good money for the property several years back, but year on year we could see our investment being blighted as the neighbour's garden deteriorated, becoming overgrown and strewn with rubbish, and those bloody trees started to block out the light and the lovely view we had over the woodland at the rear of our houses.

The local authority took no interest at all in our complaint and any attempt to impose the restrictive covenants which imposed standards for the maintenance of grounds and property via the estate management company, had also failed.

Given the dramatic changes in the level of stamp duty, a house move would be very expensive and who would want that house next door, anyway?

No, it was time for more dramatic action. Notice of the planning application was received through the post by all of the houses in the private estate. It would startle nine of the ten owners:

Elmbridge County Council
Application 34708
Nature of Application – Change of Use from Woodland to
Commercial recreation (Golf Course)
Site – Woodland Heath – adjoining Prince's Grove.
Application made by Golf Evolution Limited.

There was, of course, no prospect of the application being granted but the joy, from my perspective, was that even a ridiculous proposal needed to follow due process. This meant that it would be at least six weeks before the planning committee rejected the scheme, having canvassed the views of those who would be affected. One further bizarre quirk of planning law in England and Wales was that you don't even have to own the land upon which an application was made; a situation I intended to exploit. The extensive woodland at the rear of our garden where the golf course was proposed, was owed by The Tree Trust: ironically a charity set up to preserve the integrity of the country side.

The letter from the planning office was followed by a few days later by a flyer, said to be from Oxshott Golf Club, offering an early bird membership. Anything to enhance the credibility of the scheme.

Next, our neighbour received his first letter on the green headed paper of Golf Evolution Limited:

Dear Resident,

By now you will have received notice from Elmbridge Borough Council of our application to build a wonderful new golf course in Oxshott. Although there have been some initial concerns raised by the project, we think that the course, with its exclusive Club House, will enhance both the quality and value of your property. Locally, there has been support to the extent that we have already had interest shown by over a hundred golfers in taking out membership.

Realistically, the planning process can be a rather drawn out affair with appeals expected to both the Environmental Agency and ultimately the High Court. Your property has been identified as a site that may afford valuable access for the construction team. In these circumstances we would like to acquire from you an option to buy your property at twice its independently assessed value, if permission is granted within the next 36 months of granting this option. Although the value would be assessed at the time of acquisition, in lieu of you granting this option now, we will pay you a non-refundable sum representing 25% of the current value of your property. This value will be assessed by Stubbing Estate Agents, who are well respected in the area. As a further incentive we will allocate £5000 to enable you to present your property in the best possible light. You would also be offered £2000 to enable you to have the contract reviewed by a solicitor of your choice.

> *Should you be interested in exploring this option further, without any commitment on your part, please contact us via the link below.*
>
> *Yours Sincerely,*
> *Brian Batchelor*
> *Head of European Acquisitions*

Given that my wife was an IT marketing consultant, it had been an easy enough task to set up a credible web site complete with computer generated images of the course, which had conveniently been copied from an actual course being built in Scotland.

Even in our more optimistic moments we had not expected him to take the bait so readily, but our neighbour had expressed his interest in the option to buy within the hour. An automated acknowledgement was sent out. Time to play the hand slowly.

We let a whole week pass before the second letter was sent.

> *Dear Mr Gerrard,*
> *Oxshott Golf Club*
> *Thank you for the interest you have shown in the option to buy scheme.*
>
> *We have made a provisional appointment for the representative from Stubbs Estate Agents to visit you at home on the 26th July at 11.am in order to make an independent assessment of the value of your house. We will then formally write to you with a copy of the report and a non-refundable sum representing 25% of the assessed value.*

> *We reiterate that the sum of £5000 can be reclaimed for any work undertaken in preparation for the valuation...*

The following day, a skip arrived next door and although not wishing to be spotted watching, my wife reported a vigorous clearing up exercise in both the front and back gardens. The arrival of the gardeners a day later saw a concerted attack on the scruffy lawn and overgrown hedges. The dreaded Leylandii remained untouched.

What was needed was a further letter to Mr Gerrard.

> *Dear Mr Gerrard,*
>
> *Our surveyor has been considering the issue of site access. In order to utilise your plot it would be necessary to remove all of the trees to the rear of your property. Our concern is that there is a real danger that the Local Authority will seek to impose tree preservation orders (TPO) on those trees with a view to thwarting the development. Such a step could prove fatal to the scheme itself. At present, all of the trees are unencumbered and you are free to do with them as you see fit...*

Helen cried tears of joy as the tree fellers' vehicle drove on to the neighbour's newly weeded driveway. The sight of access ladders, chainsaws, and climbing harnesses being taken from the van was exciting, but nothing compared with the thrill of spying the first of the trees falling, cut from their bases. Five more would follow – mission accomplished bar one final letter:

18 HOLES

Dear Mr Gerrard,

Given the significant opposition to the building of Oxshott Golf Club, we have decided, not without regret, to withdraw our planning permission application. As a consequence all proposals with regards to an option to buy scheme are hereby rescinded. We know that this decision will be a disappointment for you but we hope that it has not caused any inconvenience to you...

7TH HOLE
ONE CHANCE ONLY

Only a relatively few golfers get the chance to win a Major; only an unlucky few blow the golden opportunity to do so. It was one thing to be in the hunt on the first three days of the tournament or to be the player making the late surge but that was not blowing your chance. Being three shots clear with three to play and losing – now that's blowing it. Bailey Dench fell into this camp. Bailey was a dedicated, well-liked professional on the US circuit. He had won a few minor tournaments and even just crept into the US Ryder cup team, winning the first match out on the final singles day, 5 and 4 –thereby laying a foundation for a US victory. It was the height of his career so far. He was not alone in harbouring aspirations of a shot at a big one. However, at the age of forty-two, he knew that his strength, flexibility and concentration were only heading in one direction. He relied more these days on ball and golf club technological advancements to improve his game, rather than technique. But so it was that he headed the pack by three shots going into the final round of the US Open.

His first dropped shot was hardly that, for his putt for birdie from 10 feet had been very solid from a technical perspective; no sign of fear. He had joined the crowd in their dismay as the ball hit the back of the cup and squirted out to the side. A tap in for par. His playing partner and second on the leaderboard, Hugo Cahill has been fortunate to have taken relief from a wayward drive and had then held his shortish putt for birdie with poise. *Remain positive, Bailey,* he told himself – Two up with two to play.

Their positions on the 17th green was virtually identical: Bailey to putt first for a birdie, with Cahill to follow with a shorter but certainly a missable putt. The difference this time was that Bailey's putt was a shocker; too short and as a consequence the burrow took the ball away from the hole, it was never on line. The video replay showed that it was not a case of a misread but the jerking movement of a man under pressure. He held his putt for par, just. How the crowd roared as Cahill started the putt out half a cup left and watched it drop. *Only one up one to play, but still one up!*

Cahill was a very long hitter; not always in control, but always long. His drive down the 18th found trouble, but he was lucky to be able to take relief from a television camera mast that hindered his route to the green; when your lucks in, just ride it. Bailey, sensibly listening to his long term caddie, Smithy, took his 3 wood rather than the driver. Position, not length, was the priority. This gave him the advantage of attacking the pin first and with his favoured 8 iron from 150 metres. Finding the bunker had not been a scheduled stop, especially when it was followed by a rather cautious but solid enough shot into the centre of the green from Cahill.

At this stage of the game, any shot that delivered the ball out of sand and on to the green could be viewed as a success. The NBC commentator rather summed it up as Bailey lined up his put with input from an exasperated Smithy,

"This putt to avoid disaster, but don't go anywhere just yet." The crowd were willing him to hole it; Bailey procrastinated so much that eventually they just willed him to hit it. Smithy wanted to do it for him.

The strike was solid; far too solid. The ball fired straight at the hole. It didn't drop nor stop, and the resulting two and a half feet deficit must have looked like a chasm to Bailey as Cahill secured a guaranteed playoff place with another tap in for par.

Then came Dench's turn to putt out. Some of the crowd couldn't even watch and again the TV commentator rather captured the moment.

"Well, you wouldn't want your mortgage on him holing this one, would you?"

There was a delayed reaction from the gallery as the ball lipped out. Shock, embarrassment, sympathy and indeed, support for Cahill whose final round had been impeccable. Though Dench shook hands with the victor and his caddie, he said nothing, and his eyes glazed over. To lose was one thing; to choke in doing so, and on a world stage too, unbearable. This had been his chance, the one his university coach promised he'd get.

Bailey knew that he would be fined heavily by the PGA for not giving the obligatory post round interviews, but he cared not. He went straight to the car park, ignoring all offers of condolence.

A passer-by found him; just in time to save his life but too late to avoid permanent and significant brain damage from the carbon monoxide fumes flooding his Lexus sponsored SUV. Had he only waited and carried out the painful round of media interviews, he would have heard the news. Cahill was held to have incorrectly dropped his ball when seeking relief on 18th. It was a big decision for the tournament referee to take and he reviewed the video time and time again before making the ruling. Cahill was given a two shot penalty.

Bailey Dench was the US Open champion, but would never know it.

8TH HOLE
THE HAYWARD CUP

Charles Wakefield was old school in the worse sense of the expression; sexist, racist, and homophobic for starters. He wore his club blazer and tie with pride. He had been club captain twice and a committee member for several years. He had threatened to resign when women were allowed to become full club members but, in reality, he had an eye for the ladies, too, and the thought that they could drink unfettered in the bar had its advantages. That said, as he strode towards the tee for his first round match in the club's prestigious, Hayward Cup, he had not expected to see his diminutive opponent waiting for him, resplendent in pink: skirt, top, socks and shoes.

A bloody woman – Billy indeed. Another new member we can't blackball.

"Charlie, I assume," greeted Billy as Wakefield strode towards the 1st tee.

"Charles, actually," he retorted, barely managing to make

eye contact. "I thought you were…I mean Billy and all that. Don't take this the wrong way, but I didn't think that women could play in the Hayward Cup.

"Well, Charlie, I noticed from the board of honour in the club house that no woman as ever won the trophy, but as long as everyone plays off the blue tees, it's an open competition, right?"

That should cut her down to size.

Wakefield, at least perceiving himself as an upstanding gentleman, offered Billy the honour, but in a less gentlemanly manner took an unnecessary interest as her pink skirt rode up to facilitate teeing up.

Hello, matron.

Wakefield wasted no time in probing further. Noticing no wedding ring, he enquired as they walked together up the first.

"Does your boyfriend play at all?"

"No boyfriend at the moment, I'm afraid. We split up recently."

Noted, Billy, noted.

"He was more interested in the television than me."

Silly boy

"You married, Charlie?"

"Most of the time, Billy," quipped Wakefield, reluctant to be drawn into a discussion on the breakup of his third marriage.

Wakefield was suffering from cognitive dissonance; he had always seen the game of golf as a male domain, yet was intrigued and attracted to his younger playing partner. Young, attractive and available, partner.

The thought put him off his game for the first three holes,

by which time the diminutive, but very accurate, Billy had taken the lead.

I hope she's more wayward off the course smiled Wakefield to himself. The match was pretty much tied up after the turn. Wakefield would underplay his thrashing, of course, but his intrigue outweighed any disappointment. He gratuitously patted Billy on the bottom with his putter as he conceded the 13th hole and noted no objection unlike a longer standing club member, Fiona Kilgour, who had reported him to the club secretary last year for doing just that.

Frigid cow.

As Billy held an eight-foot putt for victory, 4 and 3 on the 15th, Wakefield rushed in, rather too eagerly, for a kiss on Billy's cheeks, ignoring the victor's out stretched hand for shaking.

I'm sure she puckered her lips too.

Wakefield, to his credit, congratulated Billy on making it through to the next round of the Hayward Cup.

"We might see a woman's name on the board yet."

"Indeed we might, Charles."

"Let me buy you a drink, Billy."

"Yes, lovely, let me take a quick shower first."

Ding dong

"Good idea," rebounded Wakefield, "see you in the bar in 10 minutes." And with that, another pat on the buttock and he was heading to the men's locker room.

He whistled contently in the shower, but as he opened the shower door, there standing just two metres away, wrapped in a white fluffy towel, Billy.

Well, I say – here we go!

The towel slipped to the floor and there was Billy naked before him and looking straight at him. Small in stature, yes, but there was nothing diminutive about Billy's penis!

Wakefield rushed back into the shower cubicle, locking the door behind him – He didn't know what the club rules were for transgender players but he didn't reappear until the shower water had run cold.

9TH HOLE
MINDFULNESS

My initial thought was a negative one: miss this putt and you've lost. However, my recent mindfulness course had stressed the need to be positive in times of stress. Good advice: *lighten the grip, make a positive strike, keep your head still.*

It was difficult to focus because those watching were unquestionably unsupportive and vocal with it. Very unsporting.

Keep in the now; take your time. Think technique, not outcome. Imagine the ball dropping into the cup.

I settled behind the ball, braced my lower body, and focused on nothing but the point of impact on the ball. A smooth draw back and an accelerated putter head saw the yellow ball on its way up the first slope without complication. Next, the most challenging part, avoiding the blade of the revolving windmill.

Yes!

Into the entrance of the Helter Skelter.

Has it enough pace? It does!

Out the other side now and rolling towards the hole, missing, but with the chance of a rebound off the concrete back wall. It wasn't to be.

Game lost; family cheering and time for an ice cream along the promenade. Enough crazy golf for one day.

10ᵀᴴ HOLE
WHEEL POWER

Ryan Whitehead had been in a wheelchair since the age of 18, having been shot with a hand gun as part of an East London gang turf war. Ryan was the *tit for the tat*, for a week earlier his gang had stabbed a rival gang member. Life, as Ryan will tell you, was tough on the streets before the attack, but nothing compared with life in the wheelchair that followed as this young man returned home to the crime ridden streets that formed a major part of his community. Ryan readily describes the vulnerability as overwhelming, and the discrimination as appalling.

It was against this background that Ryan initially and to be fair, reluctantly, became involved in a scheme set up by the London Mayor to try and tackle gang violence. That venture led to Ryan's profile being raised and as his anger mellowed, he became increasingly involved in disability politics, helping to raise awareness and fight discrimination. It was a natural progression to accept an appointment to the Board of the

Spinal Injuries Trust (SIT, of all things). He even received an MBE for services to the community; Ryan had come a long way from those days of street violence.

He sat and listened politely to the SIT chairman working her way through the agenda. The issue of fund raising was always of concern and this trustee meeting was no different. Sponsorship and support for the annual ball was down and with only 6 weeks to go. Although the Grand Hotel in London gave them preferential rates to hire the ballroom, the overheads for the event were higher than usual, for what was year on year by far the biggest fund raising event of the year.

"The lawyers have not been as generous this year, and let's be honest, that bout of food poisoning last year didn't help," came the assessment from Paul Bamford the head of fundraising. Ryan chirped, "I've got an idea, Madam Chairman. I want to work with a number of golf clubs. I've received this cheque for £1000 just this morning from Mintford Park Golf Club. They have agreed to take a table at the ball too. I think that there's more I can do. Leave it with me."

Bamford was pleased to take the cheque and revise the table numbers for the Ball.

Two weeks earlier, Ryan had visited Mintford Park Golf Club in order to attend a birthday lunch of a friend. The experience was not a positive one. To start with, there were no disability parking spots, and therefore the trip across the gravel drive in his wheelchair was protracted and precarious. Access to the club house was up two sets of steps and Ryan had the choice of either being lifted up or taking a circuitous route via the first tee along an undulating track ridden with ruts and pinecones. The club said that they had a ramp somewhere, but the storeroom was locked and the club secretary who held on to the key was not due in until the next day. Access to the restaurant area was a little easier but only because the three stairs were down, not up. As a skilled wheelchair user, he was able to bump down the stairs noisily, but under control. Having opted for the longer route into the clubhouse, his wheels had become muddy, and this meant that his gloved hands were also wet and dirty; Ryan was embarrassed about the tyre trail his chair left across the club's carpet. He would need a comfort break and wanted to clean his hands before lunch. The key was eventually found for the disabled loo, but it was full with two hoovers, a child's high chair, a mop and bucket.

The restaurant manager was more defensive than apologetic, and it was this attitude that had led him to write to the Club Secretary, on official SIT headed paper, detailing his experience and referencing discrimination legislation. Ryan was not shy in highlighting his contacts with the media, but asked that in the circumstances, consideration be given to making a donation to support the forthcoming Ball. The response was a very positive one and this got Ryan thinking further.

Are all golf clubs like this? What if I actually wanted to play a round of golf too? Would they all be as keen to avoid adverse publicity? Perhaps, yes.

It was time to find out!

First, he set off to American Golf to buy a cheap pencil bag and a few clubs to put in it. To their credit, disability access from parking to payment was excellent, albeit the salesman was curious as to Ryan's expectations from his new sport. He had seen wheelchair tennis and rugby on the television, but wheelchair golf eluded him.

Ryan mapped out his tour. Three golf clubs a day should be achievable. His first visit couldn't have gone better or worse from the club's perspective. Access to the club house just wasn't a viable option, and the embarrassed club pro stood outside in the rain with Ryan explaining the problems that were self-evident.

I think that I can put them down for a table for the ball.

The second club, Downsend, in Kent, even had a disabled parking bay albeit taken up by two buggies.

It's the thought that counts…

Access to the pro shop was courtesy of the automatic doors and a breeze. The sympathetic young pro stared down at Ryan and shook his head.

"We could get you to the warm up range but you'll never make it down the wooden railway sleeper steps to the first tee…"

Maybe something for the silent auction?

Mapledown, Ryan's third visit of the day, was a revelation. Disabled parking, ramp access, and a pro happy to take a green fee. It transpired that last year's Captain had suffered a stroke during his year in office. This had resulted in a number of changes being made to facilitate easy access for Sir Reginald, of which Ryan was now the beneficiary. Given that Ryan had never hit a golf ball before, he was not about to give wheelchair players a bad name; he therefore pretended to take a call from his fictitious wife and a problem with the toilet plumbing that required his immediate attendance.

It transpired that Mapledown Golf Club was the exception to the rule as each club in turn was inspected and received from him the standard letter addressed from the Spinal Injuries Trust expressing disappointment and threatening litigation.

How satisfying it was for Ryan to receive an email from the head of fundraising.

Dear Trustees,

I am delighted to report that all tables for the forthcoming London Ball have been sold. We have also received a number of decent prizes for the auction to include a two week stay in a disability friendly villa in Italy, courtesy of Sir Reginald Firth. Thanks to Ryan for his hard work, he must have twisted a few arms along the way...

11ᵀᴴ HOLE
A VERY MODERN GAME

Gary Ballardo was resting in his bed at the Vardon Institute, Florida's leading cryogenic clinic. He was in the early stages of rehabilitation following what the Institute calls "rebirthing". Gary had been in a state of living suspension for a relatively short period, only 290 years. Rebirthing broadly involves three phases; the first, and by far the most dangerous stage, was the rapid transition from being suspended in a cubicle of liquid nitrogen at minus 196 degrees, to a body temperature of 38 degrees and the introduction of enriched oxygen via a ventilator. Throughout this period the *client*, never *patient*, remains in an induced coma. Death rates during this period had improved exponentially since the pioneering days of the technique, but the risks remain real.

The second phase, known in the industry as "the transition", was a period of significant testing and observation. Muscles were electrically stimulated, and physiotherapy robots massaged, turned, and stretched the client's limbs and spine. Cranial stimulation was introduced, but it was only towards the end of this transition phase that the first attempts were made to instigate consciousness, followed by a phased withdrawal of the ventilator.

The final phase, social rehabilitation, focuses, as the term implies, more on social than medical issues. This, too, is a challenging period. Whilst changes in economic, technological, and political issues often overwhelm, frequently the most difficult issue for the client to come to terms with is the death of loved ones, family members who were alive at the time of the cryogenic procedure. That deep sense of grief can be counterbalanced by the knowledge that the family line not only continues, but that surviving relatives are keen to meet their long-lost family member.

Gary had been assigned two holograms, Bea and Helena, whose task was to educate Gary on the significant changes that had taken place, and deal with a myriad of questions from him.

Gary's concerns switched between wars and conflicts to more positive subjects; in particular the cures for cancer, HIV and Alzheimer's. His mind turned to sport. He was staggered to be told that American Football was now a marginal sport, and his beloved Yankees had folded through insolvency. He was further surprised to be told that horse racing had been banned for cruelty, and China had been world soccer champions for three consecutive World Cups. He shook his head. As a former 15 handicapper, Gary quickly asked about his favourite pass time.

"Don't tell me golf has been banned, too!"

Bea smiled.

"It's still going strong, you'll be pleased to know, Gary. We call it H10. Ten holes only these days. In fact, it is the second and final day of the Masters today. It's being played this year at our home course here in Florida. I'll pull it up for you." And with that, the 3D visuals appeared in the room as though floating in mid-air.

The first thing Gary noticed was the crowd all dressed in white and wearing large goggles and a transparent helmet for protection.

The screen showed the first round leaderboard:

Pang Chin – 14 mins 20 seconds

Reece Murdoch – 14 mins 24 seconds

Racko Mei – 14 mins 32 seconds

Just then the crowd cheered as the next player was introduced on the tee.

"From the 52th State of the USA with a first round time of 15 minutes and 48 seconds and the current Masters Champion, Carlos Quinn." Up stepped Carlos, acknowledging the applause. He was dressed in a pink lycra one piece suit with what appeared to be a Coca Cola logo on his chest. His data appeared: 7' 2 "- 220 lbs pulse 98 – Blood pressure 150/85. He was waving a club in his hand. The camera focused on the club as he adjusted the angle of the head by pressing a remote control button. The official handed him a ball; it looked larger than the ones Gary had recalled.

Carlos placed the ball into a cylindrical pot and then the ball raised into the air, suspended, it appeared, on a stream of air. The official counted down for ten with the help of the crowd. Carlos then took a two-step run-up, struck the ball and set off running after it as the clock in the top left-hand corner begins to tick; his second round was underway. Gary watched, bemused, as Carlos struck his second shot, slowing to a jog but not stopping. He was quickly off and running again. The green had two pins in it; both flags bore sponsor logos *Chung* and *Starbucks*. Carlos chipped and nearly held out before tapping in and running to the next tee or two of ten as the commentator called it.

It was a lot to take in; better stick with the changing politics for now. And with that he dismissed the holograms and drew down his laser headphones. Gary settled down to learn about the turbulent China / US relations and the demise of the rainforest. It was depressing. Time to return to the golf. Gary asked Bea for an update.

"Who won the Masters in the end?"

In an instant, up popped the visuals, there for all to see:

With a combined winning time of 28 minutes 20 seconds from Poland the winner, Lotte Larenski.

There was Carlos Quinn helping the new Masters champion on with the green jacket. Lotte was blubbing like a baby. Apart from the *Chung* logo on the blazer, some things, reflected Gary, never change.

12ᵀᴴ HOLE
FOR THE LOVE OF THE GAME

The agency saw themselves as purveyors of pleasure, not supporters of betrayal, but their focus on unfaithful relationships was controversial none the less.

Lovers Leap was an agency with deceit at its heart. Clients were very grateful for the services offered for a monthly retainer, starting at £100 plus expenses. Clients were provided with everything from alibis to receipts to disguise their matrimonial infidelity. Lovers could book hotels, send flowers, and buy lingerie in the complete confidence that there was no audit trail for their spouse to follow. Whilst there were more men on the books, many a female executives were spicing up life with their services.

Phil Bachelor had been a platinum member for the last six months. He found the service ideal: an enriched sex life without the prospect of being caught. His life as a chief finance officer for a leading investment company also came with a public profile, and Phil was delighted with the degree of discretion the agency had shown.

His mistress and loyal PA, Caroline, was putting pressure on him for a long weekend away. Phil consulted the agency as to what options were available to him.

"I can see from your details that you don't fish, climb or shoot; a shame as all good excuses for a phone free trip. Ah, I see you like golf. Have you played recently?"

"Yes, as it happens a couple of corporate events including a recent Pro – Am."

"Great – you must be due a golf break with the boys?"

"I most certainly am!" said Phil sensing the evolution of a plan.

"Golf in say Le Touquet for the boys and trip to Paris for you?"

"Sounds just perfect – can you line it up for the weekend of the 26th?"

"No worry; I will send you an itinerary for approval by tomorrow."

Friday the 26th couldn't come around soon enough for Phil. His wife, Charlotte, had noticed his increased enthusiasm for golf in the build-up to the trip; visits to the local golf range and endless putting on the living room carpet. He had even worked late in the office to clear his desk for the trip.

Friday came. There was a toot from a car horn outside the house, followed by a ringing of the doorbell.

"That will be the boys, love. Can you tell them I'm coming?"

Charlotte briskly opened the door to be met by a jovial young chap, already dressed for 18 holes, wearing a Royal County Down tee shirt and checked blue and white trousers.

"You must be, Charlotte. I'm Mike; here to give your old man a good thrashing in France."

Charlotte shook his outstretched hand and acknowledged the other guys in the car whose arms extended out of the windows and waved in exaggerated fashion.

"Phil, time to go. The boys are waiting."

Her husband appeared carrying his holdall.

"Hi, Mike, good to go? The Chunnel's booked for 9.30? Plenty of time albeit that M20 traffic can be busy."

Phil turned to Charlotte, pecked her on the cheek and picked up his clubs. The car was not heading to Dover but to Heathrow where his lover Caroline would already be enjoying an early glass of Champagne in the business class lounge.

The first text photo from Phil to his wife was of a "Chunnel ahead" sign. It would be the first of several that had been loaded up on his phone for him; photos taken from professional library stocks or manipulated team golf group taken from golf courses and wine bars as well as individual photos of Phil enjoying his golf, taken a week earlier. The agency had certainly perfected the golf weekend: he would be supplied with his marked-up score cards from Le Touquet, a fake hotel invoice, and a hard copy team photo from outside the club house.

As Phil enjoyed the sensual luxury of the Hotel du Paris with Caroline, he had no hesitation in ordering fine wines and room service, safe in the knowledge that all billing would go via the agency's credit card.

It is difficult to say exactly what alerted Charlotte's suspicions. Certainly, she was surprised to note that he had packed his new Calvin Klein boxers which he'd bought but a week ago. And do you really take your after shave with you to play golf? *Maybe*

No, it was the group photo Phil sent via WhatsApp; there was Phil smiling in front of the clubhouse, arms around his fellow golfers, proudly wearing his favourite and distinct *Hole in One Club,* royal blue polo shirt – the very one she had found in the laundry basket this morning.

Phil made his way back in the taxi from Heathrow having been reunited with his golf clubs. He was exhausted. His biggest fear was that his wife Charlotte would want a night of passion to make up for his weekend away with the boys – On that front, he needn't have worried.

13ᵀᴴ HOLE
THE SHANK

Given the title of this chapter, the fact that you are reading it points to you either being very cruel, particularly stoic, or a non-golfer. The shank is a curse, dreaded throughout the game. Its very reference, much like Voldemort or Macbeth, should not be mentioned in polite company. There are many professional golfers who will refuse to coach those afflicted for fear that it is somehow contagious. The shank, unlike any other shot in the game, destroys players and unlike lightning, always strikes again and again.

The ability to send a ball at a 60 degree angle from a shot directed straight ahead is really quite a feat, but one rightly feared by all players. Even to observe a fellow golfer strike one off the heel causes the stomach to tighten and eye contact with the afflicted one is impossible to achieve.

From a technical perspective it is possible to analyse a cause: too close to the ball at take away? A looping swing? Defective right shoulder movement? But that is like diagnosing the plague, the cause matters little when the outcome is fatal.

So it was that Andy Kilgower drove off from the first at Bridlington Marsh Golf Club in Yorkshire a scarred man; one with this affliction: a shanker. The textbook idea that you should forget about it and focus on a more positive strike of the ball, could only have been written by someone who has never had the problem.

In case you wonder, it is possible to shank the ball with a driver, though it tends then to shoot the ball acutely to the left for the right hander. The ball will almost always be lost given the velocity of the swing, the tight angle of flight, and the close proximity of the tee to woodland or bush. The shank is harder to achieve off the larger club face of the driver, but this factual data didn't assist Andy as his ball disappeared for good. His third shot off the tee was a half swing, come punt which at least connected. Although only bumping a hundred and fifty metres or so, he was in play and everyone in the four ball let out a knowing sigh of relief.

The curse, as Tommy Gibson, the club pro, had called it, had just appeared mid round three months back. No warning, no gentle introduction, just wham – *welcome to the shank*. It was surely not without significance that the problem coincided with financial pressures at work. Golf was proving to be far from the escape activity he had hoped that it would be in adverse times.

Even Andy, who was a good-natured optimist, was seriously doubting his future in the game. No round since had been shank free. His sliding handicap was of no significance, and his regular playing partners could barely watch. Their words of wisdom were unhelpful and it is difficult to offer encouragement to a man on the cusp of disaster. Best to say nothing.

After three consecutive holes without default this morning, Andy's confidence was hardly rising, but he was starting to believe that by consciously widening his stance and standing further away from the ball, he might just have found the solution.

As his 7 iron second shot on the 14th hole disappeared sharply into the surrounding trees, hopes of a cure faded as quickly as they had appeared. A temporary remission, false hope.

Andy trudged head down into the wood having advised the others to play on without him; they were only too eager to do so. His ball was not exactly on display and he hunted further. He would not waste much time looking. Something caught his eye at the base of an adjoining rhododendron bush. He used his errant 7 iron to explore. Some form of bag or holdall, perhaps? He hooked the club around the handle and dragged it out. An army style camouflaged holdall, zipped up but clearly with something in it. Brushing away the moss and mud from the top of the bag, he unzipped the holdall, slowly at first, as though afraid of releasing the Genie, but then more rapidly as the contents came into sight.

It was stuffed with cash, orderly stored, but stuffed to the brim with filthy dosh nonetheless. Andy was too shocked to make any estimate of amount beyond noting that the used £50 notes were bound together in bundles secured by elastic bands.

Trying to think on his feet, he zipped the bag back up and pushed it even deeper under the bush. After a moment of reflection, he pulled the bag out again and pulled out several wads of cash, stuffing his trouser pockets. He laid another bundle on the ground; he would put those in his golf bag which waited patiently for him in the short rough. Andy replaced the stash under the bush. He had barely interfered with the top layer of readies.

No one noticed as he loaded up his side bag panel. The group was by now used to him playing in a parallel, shanker's universe. When he joined them on the green, they barely acknowledged his presence.

Rather bizarrely, Andy, with his mind focussed elsewhere, was able to complete his round without too many problems. Putting that in perspective, he didn't lose anymore balls, though didn't get close to a par.

As his group strolled back to the clubhouse, he pondered what he should do. There was no doubt in his mind that he would go back for the rest of the money, it was just how he did it without being seen or raising suspicion. He couldn't just stroll back on to the 13th and rummage in the bushes. It had come as no surprise to anyone when Andy said that he was going go down to the practice area to hit a few balls. The range backed on to the 13th; he would try and cut through unseen and hope that no one could possibly have hit such a bad shot so to join him in the wooded area.

It was late afternoon and the sun was already dropping. The practice area was empty, bar the yellow practice balls that littered the grass. Andy carried his Ping golf bag with him. He had emptied out the pockets and removed a few clubs too. Approaching the dividing line, he ducked under the netting that separated the range from the course. Finding the holdall again was not straight forward given that the surrounding area all looked the same: beach trees and rhododendrons bushes. Andy could see through the cluster of trees that a two ball was making its way up the fairway. Andy ducked in behind a tree out of sight. It was helpful for him to see where their drives had landed as this gave him a better gauge of where he had entered the wood. Inevitably, they would be bigger hitters than he was; he would factor that into his orienteering. The two men passed, keeping very much out of the rough, and Andy began hunting again. How he wished he left some form of marker. Was it this far in? He tried to relive his dreadful shank. Yes, it could have gone in a long way and at speed. *Look further in.* Perhaps the bag had been found by someone else or even collected…

No, not collected, thought Andy, as he spotted the treasure trove. He dragged it out and checking again that he couldn't be seen, unzipped it and began to load up his bag. It was bulging by the end and he loaded his pockets too. There would be time to count later, but there was an awful lot of money. Andy smiled as he pulled off one £50 note and placed it back in the empty bag, enough for the disappointed owner's taxi home, perhaps. He threw the bag back into the bush.

As Andy turned to walk back to the driving range he saw it nestled in a clump of long grass: his lost NXT Tour golf ball complete with his initials. He picked it up and kissed it. He hadn't cured his shank, but he would never care again.

14ᵀᴴ HOLE
YIPPIE

Tony was invited by the facilitator to stand up and introduce himself.

"Hello. I'm Tony Barrow, and I have the yips."

"Welcome, Tony," came the reply from the group of seven men in unison.

"Yes, welcome, indeed, Tony. Do you feel ready to share your story with us?" asked Dr Susan Mitchell, a clinical psychologist leading the session. The question was an open one without pressure, for Dr Mitchell knew that speaking at one's first group meeting was very challenging.

Tony sat down and rested his putter on the side of his chair. He paused to compose himself and then looking above the heads of the group began to tell of his journey.

"I can remember the exact moment as clear as day. It was a friendly round with a couple of work pals on a Saturday morning. Plenty of banter, and plenty of average golf. I was left with what looked like straight two and a half foot putt, slightly downhill. As I stood over the putt, I thought that I could see a break, half a cup left to right. I stood away, stepped back two paces and got down on my haunches to inspect further. I was taken aback at the level of ridicule I received from my playing partners for the apparent indecision. Objectively, I could see why – a short putt with nothing at stake, but it rattled me. I hurried back into position, paused for what felt like ages, and then tapped the ball feebly towards the outside left edge. The nonsense is that the ball dropped into the hole…just. The ironic cheers from the boys didn't help but I knew that something had changed for the worse."

For the first time in the session, Tony looked at the group. They acknowledged his pain, for though their tales were different, each at their core were very much alike. A trigger moment full of doubt; fear of ridicule, failure, and knowledge that the self-doubt would linger.

"Thank you, Tony, That can't have been easy for you. Are you content to tell us more?" Tony nodded to Dr Mitchell, wiped away the perspiration from his brow, and continued.

"On the next hole, a strange thing happened. I hit a super wedge in to the green, and the ball rolled just past the cup, leaving what I thought was a tap in. But as I got closer to the green, I could feel my heart start to pound; I genuinely wanted a longer putt. What if I missed this one? I marked my ball very deliberately, praying that my playing partner would give it to me. *Don't make me putt out, please.* Instant solace was granted just as I was returning to place the ball.

'Sorry, Tony, we should have said take it away. Not even you would miss that one.' If only he'd known how I felt. And here I am, two years later, desperate and humiliated."

Dr Mitchell initiated polite applause and thanked Tony for his candour.

"Let's go around the room and see how we've got on since the last session." She checked her notebook. "Reece, how was your charity purge?"

"A bit mixed, doc. Just to remind the group, if I missed a putt of under 4 feet or under, I had to make a £10 donation to my favourite charity. Put it this way, we should be able to find a cure for prostate cancer pretty soon!"

"Did you *feel* any different?" asked another of the afflicted, interested in the idea.

"Yeah, I did to be honest. Nice that someone was benefiting from my incompetence. I'm going to stick with it 'til the next session, but I might up the stake to £20 in order to focus the mind."

Julian put his hand up indicating that he was ready to report. Dr Mitchell gestured to him.

"Hypnosis for me. Don't laugh, my putting is still dreadful, but I haven't had a smoke for a month."

The group laughed, enjoying the light relief. Just then, the door to the church hall opened noisily, disturbing the intimacy of the group. In stepped a middle-aged woman.

"Come in, Gilly," encouraged Dr Mitchell, clearly expecting the visitor. Whilst the men assumed that Gilly was a fellow yips sufferer, Dr Mitchell directed her to the adjoining ladies toilets.

"You can get dressed in there, Gilly. We will be ready for you in five minutes." Gilly thanked Dr Mitchell and waved to the seated group.

"See you all in 5."

Dr Mitchell called the group to order.

"Guys, we are going to experiment with positive imagery today. Gilly is a life model from the art school and will be helping us. I've set up the putting mat, so bring your putters and line up please. Collect a couple of balls each on the way."

Tony as the newest member of the group, was invited to head the queue as Gilly reappeared from the ladies toilets dressed in a red rope and made her way over to the green baize putting mat. To the amazement of the queuing yipsters, Gilly undid her robe and stood there in matching blue satin knickers and bra. Without hesitation, she stepped over to the end of the mat and sat down, shuffling on her bottom until she sat spread-eagled aside the raised soft rubber hole, one leg on each side. It was quite a sight.

"Putts from 3 feet, please, to start with. Tony, you kick us off."

Tony was far from comfortable, but took solace from Gilly's smiling face. She encouraged him.

"I'm used to being part of a living sculpture, but this is new I must say," said Gilly unfazed.

Tony hit his first putt straight into the waiting cup. He had felt a familiar tightening of his body as he took his up his stance, but was less sure whether that was the yips or embarrassment. The sufferers took it in turns.

"Not too hard, Brian," called Dr Mitchell, slightly alarmed at one of the player's enthusiasm." After 15 to 20 minutes, Dr Mitchell signalled an end of the experiment and led a round of applause for Gilly. The feedback session was positive. The test now would be to picture Gilly on the course itself, when facing a tricky putt.

Tony had to wait until the third hole of his weekend round for his first short putt of the day. He closed his eyes for a moment, smiled, and stroked the putt firmly home without hesitation.

15ᵀᴴ HOLE
Q SCHOOL

When I arrived at Florida State University on a golf scholarship from the UK, I was the best player, not only of that year's fresher intake, but of all the students on the three-year golf program. Playing off *plus 4* and fresh from success in the English Amateur Open, I was on the cusp of great things. Not my words, but those of the BBC. Things changed.

To plagiarise George Best and John Daly, I spent most of my time and money on women and booze, but I wasted the rest. I was away from home for the first time with money in my pocket from sponsorship support and through the scholarship itself. I had the pick of the US universities and Florida had been the most generous. Although I was there to play golf, the campus was full of young people not looking to develop a professional sports career, but just have a good time. I joined them.

Whilst back in the UK, I had spent every spare moment spent practicing, hour after hour. But now, I couldn't wait for the daily and obligatory coaching sessions to be over so I could either recover from the night before or plan the one ahead. Oh, and how those American students loved my accent.

Talent can only get you so far; it's the combination of talent and hard work that produces results. We all know that, but implementation is another thing. I was so talented that I cruised through the first year. Representing the university, winning tournaments and feeling invincible. The downturn was imperceptible at first. It always starts with the drives and long irons where the margin for technical error is so small. When you are generating club heads speed of 110 mph, even being a couple of degrees off centre at impact can mean the difference between the fairway and the long rough. You are then trying too hard to recover, and by the time you get to the dance floor, you're under pressure to avoid a bogey, let alone make a birdie.

And so it is that I end up back in the UK for my third and final year at Q School. There was a limit on how long you can keep trying, and this at the age of only 28, was it. Paradoxically, in many ways it is harder to obtain a professional license through Q School than it is playing tournament golf. Every player at this stage is desperate to succeed and this is the final opportunity of the season to gain that golden ticket. The pressure was really on me this year; sponsors had fallen away, and a benefactor who had supported my career throughout had finally lost patience and withdrawn his annual stipend; his dream of backing a Major winner in tatters.

The format at Q School was straight forward: two rounds, top 5 qualify to play on the professional circuit next season. Qualifying took place at three courses. I had chosen

Claremont Hill, given that I had played it many times and knew the nuances of the tricky greens as well as any local caddie. The choice appeared to have been paying off because at the end of day one, my name was firmly towards the top of the leaderboard. A two under par 70 put me in joint third place, only two shots off the lead but with a Q alongside my name. The letter meant nothing on day one, but it would sure be valuable tomorrow. My confidence was high. I was striking the ball well and had my putting been more spectacular, I would have been at the top of the board.

I needed a beer to unwind. I knew from experience that there was no point in heading to bed for an early night. Sleep mid tournament was always scarce. Better to unwind and if anything, stay up a bit later. I headed down to the hotel bar. The hotel I had chosen to stay was not the closest to the course, nor the cheapest either, but I wanted some home comforts even if funds were running low. Perhaps, not surprisingly, there was not another pro in sight. That was how I liked it. The idea of talking golf with a group of self-doubters, an attitude that epitomises Q School, had no appeal. The bar was still relatively lively, with people already winding down for the weekend. A noisy group of young men in suits but no ties were complimented by a quieter cluster of women enjoying what looked to be a Prosecco and a catch up.

I was happy to enjoy a pint of draught *Peroni* and sit at the end of the bar with my ear pods and a catch up on the my favourite podcasts. It would take my mind off tomorrow's challenge. One beer led to two more, at which stage I thought that I needed something to eat and ordered the minute steak sandwich with some fries—the stuff of which champions are made.

It was not the raised voices that caught my attention, for the iPhone earpieces were of excellent quality, but the movement to my right and the reaction of the barman who I could see from my peripheral vision. I looked up and unplugged as I witnessed what could only be described as an altercation between an older chap who I had not noticed previously and several of the tieless lads. The girls were all standing now and seemed to be acting as peacekeepers. The older chap, balding and dressed in smart casuals, was in his sixties, I'd say. I rather assumed that he had stepped out of line with the girls and the 'suits' had stepped in gallantly to assist; credit where it's due.

It was clear though from the barman's intervention that I had miscalled it. It was visa versa: Baldy was the hero and I watched as two of the suits apologized for the conduct of their other colleague, who was by now being restrained by his friends, clearly the worse for wear. I tried to keep out if it, for it was not my fight, but as the right hook struck the gallant older chap's nose and spread across his face, there came a shriek of alarm from one of the women – enough was enough. I peeled myself off the stool just in time to stop the second blow reining in. I now became the target for abuse as one of the lads threw the balance of their larger over me, indicating in no uncertain terms that this wasn't my fight. Instinctively, I stuck out a right jab, catching the abuser smack on the end of his jaw. Even if I say so myself, it was a beauty. He went out like a light and was caught by his pals as he headed groundward. The bar man shouted that he was calling the police and it brought everyone to their senses again. I put my arm around the shoulder of the victim who was clutching his nose and led him into the toilets to freshen up.

Reg, as he then introduced himself, was very grateful, yet apologetic for having got me involved.

"No respect for anyone, some people."

I let Reg clean himself up and I discretely checked out the bar. The threat of police presence had cleared out the assailants and victims alike. I gave Reg the all clear and he headed to the nearby lift, looking to adjourn for what had been a far too adventurous evening. As he thanked me again, he shook my hand with vigour, and I winced realising for the first time that my impeccably delivered punch had injured the knuckles on my right hand. I headed back to the bar to get some ice for the swelling. The barman offered me a further pint on the house, and I departed with beer, ice bucket, and battered tin tray to my room. As the adrenaline wore off, the pain increased. The ice would aid the swelling, but what if there was any underlying damage? It was a mistake to pull out my 7 iron from the bag propped up against the wardrobe, for I could barely grip it. It spooked me, and had it not been for the beer/ Ibuprofen combo I would not have slept at all.

The morning brought little solace, for although the swelling had reduced a little, the pain had increased. What an idiot. An entire career at risk through a moment of chivalry. I had a late tee off time, and this enabled further icing. Had it not been for the tournament, an X-ray would surely have awaited me.

I kept my warmup to a minimum with a greater focus on the putting green; I was very worried. Ironically, my initial fear, that gripping the club would be a problem, proved to be unfounded. If anything, by forcing me to grip more gently, the swing was smoother. Tension always begins with the grip and though that is easy to know a fact, its implementation can be challenging.

I had been playing very steadily on level par when with a decent slice of luck, I holed out with a nine iron on the 10th. The portable leaderboard showed me in 2nd place, right in contention. Though I was trying to control the pain, the finger began to swell again. I had forced myself to endure the pain, but I was now finding that on the point of impact, I was twitching in anticipation of the acute stabbing pain that would follow. The swing became less fluid and distance restricted. The only way I could alleviate the pain was to alter my grip. In closing the grip, I could reduce contact with the knuckles, but with it brought the risk of a hook.

The risk quickly turned to reality despite trying to shape my swing more in to out. Within four holes of my good fortune, the leaderboard showed me having dropped to 5th place. This would be good enough to obtain my pro licence, but my game was falling apart and there were two players within one shot of my score. They were playing in the two ball ahead of me, so at least I would know what was needed. I'd revert to my regular grip and at least hit the ball straight. Once on the green, the throb was forgotten and my impairment incidental.

As I walked towards the 18th my hand was aching, but a par would see me secure my professional card. The drive was a bit of a blur, but either through incompetence or disability, the hook kicked in. Even my playing partner, who was not in contention, cried out in frustration as the ball curved left. I was in trouble.

The ball disappeared around the first cluster of trees spinning viciously right to left.

"Is it open out there?" I enquired of no one in particular.

"Open Andrew, but close to OB I fear – play a provisional, I would." How I belted that provisional; no pain, just anger. It flew miles, not straight, but how it flew. Its ultimate whereabouts was of no meaning now. I could barely breathe as we made our way up to the end of the cluster of trees that had hidden the ball from view. As soon as we passed the small copse it was in sight, a hundred metres off but looking very close to the wire boundary fence. Was it in or out?

Fuck it. Fuck it!

It was out. The ball had come to rest just under a section of curled up perimeter fencing that over time had unfurled from its base.

"It's out, isn't it?"

"Sorry, Andrew, it is?" replied my playing partner sympathetically.

The scorer who had been attached to our pairing also offered commiserations. I looked again at the ball, and along the fence, which ran for the better part of eighty metres each side before the next wooded area. I noted that there were two out of bounds posts at either end of this open stretch; putting aside the fencing, the ball was arguably, with a tail wind, half a ball in play.

"Andrew, I can see what you're thinking and why, but come on. Let's go and play your provisional and putt the living daylights out of it." Fighting talk, but I knew that playing three off the tee would see an end to my professional career in its infancy. I turned to the scorer.

"Can you call up the referee on your walkie talkie?"

"Sure, that's partly what it's there for."

Roger, my playing partner, shook his head almost embarrassed at my desperation.

"Tournament referee; tournament referee, this is match 21 – ruling required 18th hole at the 150 yard maker post; I repeat…"

A pause then a crackle was followed by a clear acknowledgment.

"Match 21, match 21 this is the tournament referee. Situation noted. I am currently heading over from the adjoining 15th and will be with you imminently." As if by magic, a buggy appeared through the semi rough on the other side of the fairway and headed towards us. I looked down again at the ball and concluded that the position looked pretty desperate. The scorer went to greet the referee and outline the position.

"Let's take a look for you, Mr Dinsmore. Is it in or out of play?"

I looked up rather plaintively. The tournament referee was certainly more formally dressed than when I last saw him, and his nose looked in better shape than it had done in the hotel bar. Our eyes met; no one watching would have discerned the almost imperceptible exchange.

Reg surveyed the ball, lifted the wire fencing a couple of times, and looked down the line at the white posts. He seemed to take an eternity before announcing with much pomp and authority:

"Ball in play. Obstructed by man-made hazard. Free drop, two club lengths Rule 8. 5 applies. Anything else Mr Dinsmore?"

"Thank you, sir, appreciated."

Reg even stopped to watch my 8-iron hit the green and roll but two metres past the pin. Two pain free putts for my professional card.

16TH HOLE
A LONG SHOT

As an engineering undergraduate student and keen middle-distance runner, Loughborough University was a natural home for Stephen Rooks' post-graduate doctorate. It struck him that sports biomechanics provided his opportunity to develop a viable career in sport, for realistically, he knew that he wasn't going to be good enough to earn a crust on the athletics circuit. A place in the Scottish Commonwealth Games team for the 3000-metre steeple chase impressed his friends and family, but it would not pay for a future mortgage.

His doctorate focused on the development of prosthetic racing blades for Paralympians. It was a combination of assessing materials, fittings, and in particular, ergonomic integration. How best to utilize the prosthetic cadence, stride, and body angle. Testing increasingly involved computer modelling and animation, but there was no substitute for working with the amputees in person. Given Loughborough's worldwide reputation for sporting excellence and with its first-class facilities, volunteers were not in short supply; that in itself a novelty for a research student.

Stephen, enjoying the more relaxed training regime of the winter season, had enjoyed a few beers in the student union bar and was tv channel surfing as he lay on his bed in the confines of campus. He caught the end of the football and dipped into the news before stumbling upon the golf channel. Golf was not his game, but before he flicked on to another channel, he noticed that this was not tournament highlights that were being shown but it transpired, the *US Longest Drive* competition. He watched, as much to the boisterous crowd's delight, some well-built, well dressed golfers unleashed their drivers. The distances being achieved sounded impressive even to Stephen's untrained eye. The leaderboard said it all:

1. Joe Hinks USA 345 metres – club head speed 126 mph
2. Billy Foster USA 338 metres – club head speed 128 mph
3. Brian Caldwell Jr USA 336 metres – club head speed 129 mph

Intrigued, Stephen googled how these distances and club head speeds compared with the tour professionals; the results were interesting. What surprised Stephen was that the world's top tournament players on the money list didn't feature on the list of the longest pro tour drivers. Further, the distances being achieved by the tour big hitters fell significantly short of those being featured on his late night screen. Stephen continued to watch and realized that as competitors often failed to keep their balls within the defined driving zone, that the issue for the real professionals was control and consistency. What was the point of a 300 metre drive if it ended up deep in the long grass?

Stephen was tired, but watched long enough to observe, to his surprise, the level of the prize money. $200,000 for the winner. Nice money for one shot, albeit a monster.

The next morning, Stephen made his way to the engineering block. As usual, he took a short cut through the athletics stadium cutting across the track. It was always quiet at this time of day, save a few stretching runners or a groundsman on his mower. Down the far end of the track lay the javelin runway, where today a lone figure was rehearsing his javelin launch without actually releasing the spear. Clearly satisfied with his preparation, the thrower paced out a number of steps, turned, accelerated, and launched. The power generated was so great that the javelin vibrated in mid-air before diving towards the ground and puncturing the grass out field. Stephen was impressed even if the thrower wasn't, judging from his body language. It got Stephen thinking.

I'll do some math when I get to the block. It occurred to him that, paradoxically perhaps, golf was very unlikely to be the sport that could produce the best cohort of competitors for the longest driver challenge: Wasn't the obvious choice an athletics field thrower. Putting aside the technical elements of striking the ball, all the attributes for the throws would be assets: the height, the strength, the speed, and power.

Of the three field throw disciplines, javelin, hammer, and discus, it was the latter, Stephen concluded, that afforded the most potential. Stephen would need to do the maths first, and a bit of YouTube browsing. He watched some clips from the Olympic discus final, plotting data into the computer.

The discus weighs 2 kg; the World record, 74 metres. The flight trajectory around 35 degrees. The height of release was about 1.8 metres. Friction coefficient for the discus, unsure at present but guesstimate, 2.4. Wind speed plot for 5mph assist. Gravity ratio of 1.4. What then was the velocity at the point of release the equivalent of the point of impact with the ball? ... Wow, that's impressive; John Daly, eat your heart out!

Persuading the varsity discus team to assist with his trials was not as straight forward. Stephen sold it to them on the basis that he thought that he could add a further 2 metres to their personal best performances. Combine that incentive with his biomechanics credibility, complete with computer and video equipment, and the team was on board.

The driving range in Leicester seemed a sensible place to start. Stephen's heart sank as each of the three volunteers, having taken up position in their booths, began to try and fire off a few balls. The results were dreadful. The balls were missed, the ground was hit and even when there was a connection with the ball, it was equally likely to shoot off and hit the side screen. The balls were bouncing around like a fired bullet in a metal beer barrel. Everyone, save Stephen, laughed because they had quickly realised that their dream of a resulting personal best discus throw looked to be an unlikely outcome from this session. Just then, Harry Burke, the British University's discus Champion *caught one*. One handed with a one-step lead in, he connected with all the speed and power that his discus training could muster. Although the range had distance markers from 50 – 250 metres, Stephen was unable to actually measure the shot because it sailed comfortably over the netting that designated the end of the range. There was more laughter, but now with more optimism. Stephen had a plan.

It was over a year later that Stephen touched down at Florida's Orlando International Airport. Sitting beside him across two seats was Vladimir Koch, the current Latvian discus champion and bronze medallist at the recent world championships. He was a monster of a man. At 6 '8" he weighed in at 23 stone. He could bench press 210 lbs and Squat 310lbs. And although the world didn't know it yet he could hit the golf ball further than anyone on the planet… occasionally.

17TH HOLE
CASH IS KING

HM Revenue had been suspicious about the money laundering activities of Stratham Golf Club in Hertfordshire for a good while. They had noticed that the club had been bought and sold on three occasions in the last 18 months. On each occasion, the price had increased significantly, and the new owners were always an offshore trust and thus it was impossible to know who were the individual beneficiaries.

The purported profits generated by the club were substantial and disproportionate. This, at a time when the game, generally, was struggling to attract members and the Revenue records showed that there were many clubs becoming insolvent, let alone being able to enhance profitability year on year. Stratham was certainly an outlier. The club's web site was impressive, flaunting an exclusive, members only, environment. No visitors unless playing with a member. Though there was a membership enquiry section, there were no fees listed. Members had the option of fine dining and there were corporate conference facilities available. The gallery section of the web site displayed an impressive range of photos; manicured greens, deep golden bunkers, wildlife roaming at dusk, and members enjoying the conviviality of the spiked bar.

The club's accountant didn't afford the tax inspectors much comfort either. Alex Kristov was dual-qualified here and in Belarus. His listed speciality was "international tax." He too seemed to have little interest in attracting new clientele. So it was as much with surprise as intrigue that Nigel Terrington, Senior Revenue Investigator, received a letter of invitation to meet with Kristov and his client at the golf club. The invitation followed on from a series of increasingly terse exchanges regarding the company accounts. It was not unusual for the Inspectorate to meet with professional advisors, but such meetings usually took place in high rise, glass façade blocks in the city. A visit to the actual place of work was a rarity and fraught with danger for the taxpayer, particularly the money launderers. For example, a Revenue visit to an empty warehouse in Essex for an import-export business that purports to be turning over £200,000 a week spells only one thing: a prosecution. They would accept the invitation.

"You play a bit of golf don't you, Richards? Fancy a jaunt up to leafy Herts?" enquired Terrington of his junior.

"Great. Is it a Pro-Am? No, Richards, you won't even need your clubs but, you can help suss the place out with me,"

Two weeks later, Terrington and Richards promptly arrived at the club entrance by taxi, having got the train up from Kings Cross station. They were greeted by an electric barrier, manned in an adjoining booth by an elderly chap in green blazer and tie. Terrington lowered the window.

"Nigel Terrington and Gary Richards here to meet with Alex Kristov and Christopher Handley." The gatekeeper looked down at his clip board and had to turn a page before pointing successfully at their names.

"Ah, here we are. Welcome gentlemen. Carry on around the drive, I will call ahead."

"Are you busy today?" enquired Terrington, already starting to probe.

"It's always busy, sir. Even mid-week. We hosted a conference here last week and you could hardly move." Terrington raised his eyebrows in surprised acknowledgement of the activity. They meandered around the drive to the rather grand mock Tudor mansion club house. On route they passed the car park. The men from the Revenue couldn't help but observe the range of luxury and executive cars. Range Rovers side by side with the Porsche Cayenne's. The Bentley looked impressive, as did the Aston Martin DB 11 that was undergoing a wash and polish from the two mobile car valet workers.

As the taxi pulled to a halt on the gravel drive, Alex Kristov and Christopher Handley, the club's general manager, were there to greet them. The men from the Revenue shook hands politely but lacked the enthusiasm of their hosts. Just then, they were disturbed by the noise of a helicopter that appeared over the far end of the car park and hovered before dropping down out of sight.

"We had some difficulty in getting planning permission for the helipad, but it has been a wonderful success, used every other day or so. Come, gentlemen, let me show you around before we sit down."

They were led up the steps and brought through the oak panelled doors. Turning left, the men headed to the pro shop which was well stocked with clubs and clothing. One member was trying out a new putter, whilst the other was torn between the sky-blue Pringle jumper or the richer blue top, each complete with club crest. The assistant club pro was busy checking in the 11.30 two ball.

"Is Tom around, Pete?" asked the general manager, enquiring as to the whereabouts of the senior pro.

"He's tied up with lessons until 1.00pm, Mr Handley. Shall I tell him you were looking for him?"

"No worry, Pete. Are there plenty out on the course?"

"Very steady. I could get you on just after lunch, perhaps," said Pete, looking helpfully at the tax inspectors.

"No, thank you all the same," came the swift reply from Terrington. Richards felt a tinge of disappointment.

"We would like to extend the changing area to build a spa with swimming pool, but again the planners are being short sighted." Terrington's research has indeed shown that such plans had been submitted but rejected last year.

"We have been trying to create a luxury country club feel rather than it just being about the golf. More than half our dining guests never play the game," gushed Handley with enthusiasm.

As if on cue the chef appeared in the corridor, clearly in a hurry.

"Bonjour, Henri. What's the special for lunch today?"

"Bonjour, Monsieur Handley. Aujourd'hui c'est game terrine starter and duck breast with cranberry sauce pour le main – magnifique." He kissed his fingertips as if the emphasise the quality, and with that he was gone.

"Maybe we can tempt you later," said Kristov aimlessly, for he already knew the answer; as did Richardson.

"I'll show you the restaurant on the way to the offices. Let's cut through the spike bar first."

The more informal area was manned by a barman donning the regulation green staff tie. There was fresh filtered coffee on the bar and a table of four men, dressed impeccably for a round of golf. They sat enjoying what looked to be bacon rolls. Opposite them were a group of four ladies laughing loudly and foregoing the bacon roll for a an early glass of bucks fizz .

"Morning, Christopher, join us for a bit of breakfast?" asked one of the ladies as she clinked glasses with her friend. Handley waved in mock horror but kept walking through to the main restaurant where he paused for his guests. The restaurant was surrounded by oak panels many with gold leaf inscriptions of trophy winners. Richardson noted that they were all up to date to include this year.

"We can serve thirty covers in one sitting," reported Handley proudly. He waved to the six gentlemen in the corner all wearing blazer and tie.

"British legion monthly meeting," remarked Handley casually as the full English breakfasts made their way to the table. "They've never played the game, but we are proud to welcome them." Handley pulled over one of the waiters as he returned from the table.

"Can we have some tea, coffee, and perhaps some pastries and mixed toast out front please?"

He headed to the patio doors, which opened up on to a view of the 18th Green. Adjoining the green was the practice putting area where two women golfers had parked their buggy and were looking to limber up with a few practice putts.

The men took up seats with the tax inspectors being

afforded the view. The refreshments arrived and Handley poured. As Richardson pulled out his notebook, the first of the days finishing groups made their way up the 18th fairway. Richardson, a 12 handicapper himself, noted the accuracy of the approach shots with both golfers hitting their approach shots into the green's fringe. The business meeting got underway and Richardson tried not to be distracted by the putting out.

The meeting itself was cautious: the Revenue not wanting to express their money laundering concerns, and the Club seeking to limit their tax liabilities. Chess, with consequences.

Unsurprising therefore, the outcome was not definitive. Alex Kristov conceded at the meeting that, *upon reflection*, part of the income set aside for capital expenditure was liable for corporation tax, and that the Revenue's disputed VAT estimate would not be appealed after all. The request for further trading documentation was also conceded; both Terrington and Richards were rather pleased with their day's work. The Club's accountancy still left room for significant improvement, and there was no doubt in their minds that tax evasion was perhaps more avoidance – The former criminal the later strategic. For all that, here was a thriving business; golf was alive and well at the exclusive end of the Home Counties.

"Are you sure that you won't stay for the duck special?" Richardson would have done so, but Revenue rules were tight on entertaining; so much so, that even the offer of an executive car to the station was declined.

The exit barrier raised and the doorman doffed his cap to bid farewell. Returning to his booth, he picked up the walk-in talkie.

"That's a wrap. That's a wrap."

18 HOLES

The fire alarm was sounded briefly in the club house to announce to the actors that their role playing was at an end. The exercise may have cost £100,000 inclusive of car rentals for the car park but was well worth it, given the degree of money laundering actually being facilitated through the club. The helicopter was actually Kristov's, so that reduced the expense. Finding the actors proved far easier than had been anticipated; the recruits were simply told that they were helping to show two potential investors what the club could look like if fully funded. Most would have complained to their union had they known the truth or more likely, charged a higher rate for their services.

The hardest part was finding the actors to play golf on the 18th hole. These had to be provided with a change of clothing so that they could play the hole three times in quick succession whilst the meeting took place. They simply putted out and then sneaked back on to the last hole and started again.

As Kristov congratulated Christopher Handley, alias Martin Meade the actor, the men were met my Chef Henri, whose impeccable French accent had slipped to that of a rather posh English gentleman.

"Good man; all went well I'd say, old boy. I was desperately worried that they may have actually ordered the special. Au revoir for now and all that nonsense."

Not only would an order of the terrine or duck have created a crisis, so would a request to inspect the course further, let alone play a few holes; for the 18th and the 1st were the only holes that were maintained, the others have had fairways like the rough at Carnoustie and moss ridden greens. A sad decline, but one that kept down overhead and increased the tax free profits.

18ᵀᴴ HOLE
WIN SOME, LOSE SOME

Betting on golf is big business. Even besides the larger tournaments, there were golf betting markets across the globe every week. The problem, from a punter's perspective, was that golf was, as we all know to our cost, a difficult game to predict; let alone master. The introduction of spread betting, and in particular the ability to bet on an individual player to lose, transformed the gambling options and with it the ability to manipulate markets. That's where I come in – as a betting manipulator; an illegal one at that.

The problem, from my perspective as a fixer was that the betting companies monitor irregular betting patterns. It would be easy enough to bribe an up and coming player on the minor tours; one who needed to fund his early career, or perhaps a well-known player on the senior's tour who became accustomed to the high life but didn't now have the income to pay for it. However, a large bet, one which covered the cost of the bribe and the risk of the prison sentence, would immediately attract attention and the bookie would refuse to pay out.

It was against this background that the plan was hatched to bring off a significant betting coup in the largest Major of all, the Masters in Augusta. Betting on this event ran to millions of dollars every hour of the four-day event. You could bet on everything from the number of holes in one to the score for the cut or perhaps the number of bogeys on the difficult 12th hole. Above all, you could bet substantial sums without triggering the artificial intelligence systems that monitored such markets for the large betting organisations.

The plan was simple enough: wait until the final round when there was greater clarity of outcome; when betting had become consolidated on two or three players and then strike. Corrupting or threatening the players would be the most direct of methods but the players themselves were well protected, especially those high-profile ones who were likely to be tournament leaders. This made any threat or interference with them difficult and therefore risky. What then of their families? Some travelled with the players, but those staying at home always had extra protection. Yes, over the years, attempts had been made to bribe players directly, but this had not really been a success. The good players didn't need the money, and a good living could be earned by the world's top 200 players.

But the caddies; there was nothing for them. They were just incidentals with a walk on part. Their role was often underestimated but not by us. The caddies and their families were the key to the sting. They were easy to identify, as were their homes..

Why kidnapping is not more widespread remains a mystery to most parents. It may simply be that many potential kidnappers have yet to experience the bond of parenthood and have no idea that a mother or father will do anything, absolutely anything, for the wellbeing of their children. Accepted that the act itself was cruel, penalties were high and the odds of something going wrong from capture to release not favourable. But it was guaranteed to produce a result; ask the South American drug cartels.

Our primary difficulty was knowing who the leader of the Masters would actually be. This element was essential to the sting and meant that we had to select a number of players who were in with a chance of success. Setting issues of morality to one side, practically, it was simply impossible to organise an effective kidnap plan for up to half a dozen families. It had to be the threat rather than the reality of harm that produced the desired result.

At the end of the third day's play, much to our pleasure and relief, there was not only a clear leader, but one of our six pre-selected targets. A three-stroke lead heading into the final round couldn't guarantee victory but this was the joy of in – play betting. One didn't need to wait the final outcome, as there was plenty of money to be made along the way.

Joe Tuke topped the leaderboard. He had nerves of steel and a putter that, they say, in its spare time substituted as a magic wand. His odds of winning had been cut to even money by the main stream bookmakers; this meant that for every dollar bet, the winnings would also be a dollar plus the original stake. It meant, from our perspective, that when Tuke lost, and he surely would, we, having placed bets from around the globe of him losing, would cash in.

Mickey 'Boy' Browne had been Tuke's caddie for nearly a decade. When he was not on the circuit, which was often for twenty-five weeks of the year, he was a family man. An absent father, but without doubt, a committed one. We would test that commitment. He lived in a modest house in Illinois with his wife, Gillian, and two children, Carol, aged 6 and Craig, aged 8. They were joined by an apparently friendly boxer dog called Buster.

At 8.00 pm Eastern Time a text was sent to Mickey Boy Browne; it was concise,

"Outside your house we have parked a red saloon registration plate YG 9101. In the boot, your wife, Gillian, will find a loaded pistol and a telephone number. Unless by 9 pm EST she texts the message '‛Understood' to that number, a gun identical to the one in the boot will be used in the abduction of either Carol or Craig.

Upon receipt of Gillian's reply, you will then be given your further instructions. We are watching you. If you involve the police, there will be no further discussion."

Every one of the previously selected six players' caddies had a car outside, or close, to their house with a gun and telephone number in the boot. They had been put there before the tournament began but would have blended in with the local surrounds without drawing undue attention. It just so happened that Tuke was the unlucky tournament leader.

There then ensued what we thought would be a tense wait as the hour ticked down, but far from it; for within six minutes of the text, came the reply.

"Understand but please, please leave my family alone. You must have the wrong person."

A message was sent back to Mickey straight away.

"Carry one club too many in the bag tomorrow and don't tell Tuke until AFTER the third hole but BEFORE teeing off on

the forth. If you cooperate, you will never hear from us again and your family will be safe. Your wife should once again text 'Understood' within the hour."

Again, within minutes, the "Understood" text was received. The idea of involving the caddie's wife was psychologically strategic. Left to his own devises Mickey might panic, call the police, or tell the tournament leader. But by sharing the problem with his wife, maternal instinct would prevail. Gillian would get him to swear not to tell the police. He would yield to her weeping, desperate voice; unable as he was to comfort her from over a thousand miles away.

It was time to notify our paymasters who would begin to bet against the hot favourite Tuke on accounts set up in Asia, Europe, and the States. No bet so large as to attract attention, but a steady accumulation overnight, and the next morning before play began. This financial exposure was certainly not risk free; what if Mickey Boy was prepared to call our bluff, and it was a bluff. If you the reader thought that we would kidnap innocent children, shame on you.

Our big bets would not be placed until we were sure that Mickey was carrying fifteen clubs; one more than was allowed. As long as it wasn't spotted before Tuke teed off, then his defeat would follow given the two shot penalty was per hole played with the excess club load. Punitive for a club that wouldn't be used anyway.

Checking whether or not Tuke's caddie was compliant was not without difficulty. We had two men placed down at the practice area and on the first tee. His round would be screened live and we had set up cameras to photograph the bag and enlarge the shot to check for the extra club. The only other extraneous factor was the general public. There was an increasing trend towards golfers watching at home ringing in to report breaches of the rules; a ball replaced incorrectly being the favourite, but extending to improving lies and inappropriate drops. An early call from an eagle-eyed golfing geek could bring us financial disaster.

The call from the practice ground wasn't conclusive. Mickey Boy had placed a towel over half of the bag to clean the clubs as they were discarded by Tuke in his warm-up. It was impossible to tell if this was Mickey being efficient or surreptitious.

Those members of the team situated by the first tee couldn't make their minds up either. They took several close-up photographs of the bag and emailed them through to us, but they would need wait for them to be blown up on the laptop. We sat, downloaded and magnified.

Taking into account that the putter had its own side pouch, we began to count. The top of the umbrella interrupted a clear view.

Was there a club tucked in behind it? If so, that would be the magic number – 15.

We needed a different angle view; it soon came through. Yes, there was the additional gap wedge adjoining the umbrella handle head. *The illegal fifteenth club. Game on!* We rang in to report our definitive finding. By the time we had done so, Tuke had driven long and straight down the first fairway and was on his way to a birdie start; that was even better for more frenzied betting. As long as we could survive until the third hole, the money was safe for even if it were physically possible to survive and recover from a six-shot penalty, psychologically, Tuke would be finished.

The odds shortened on his victory as every shot passed. Those in the hunting pack were making no inroads and Tuke was one under for the round and growing in confidence. He seemed to be enjoying his role as champion elect, rather than yielding to the pressure.

Mickey would surely report his misdemeanour as instructed. He would want to secure his family's safety. As the players walked towards the 4th tee, we watched excitedly as Mickey reached into his bag and pulled out a club. It was clearly not the driver that Tuke would need next. There was then a protracted discussion between the clear tournament leader and his caddie. Mickey then handed him up a mobile phone. The television commentator could hardly contain himself.

"The tournament leader is on his mobile phone – can you believe it?

His caddie, Mickey Boy Browne, looks apprehensive, perhaps he fears disqualification for contacting an outside agency? Michael you are our rules guru – are you allowed to use a phone?"

"Quite an unusual sight, isn't it? There is nothing in the rules to specifically say that you can't use your phone on the course, but you are not allowed outside assistance. It would be a two-shot penalty to ask a friend on the phone how far a putt breaks, for example. The match referee could also rule it to be ungentlemanly conduct which is penalised with a fine not a shot penalty."

"The saga continues because Tuke has now handed his phone to his caddie; maybe he forgot to turn the oven off this morning, perhaps the credit card bill needs paying; who knows?" mocked the commentator. The golfer and his

caddie stopped walking as Mickey finished the call. The two then engaged in conversation, seemingly oblivious to their surroundings.

"They'll be done for slow play next. Quite extraordinary. It looks like quite a row."

"Maybe they need reminding that they are in the middle of one of the world's biggest golf tournaments, being watched by millions around the globe. Oh, hang on: this looks like progress. The caddie has put away the gap wedge and pulled out the driver." The move brought ironic cheers from the rather bemused crowd crammed into the stand adjoining the tee. Tuke, seemingly mindful of the furore he was causing, took no time with prepping his drive. Not even a practice swing. When you are on your game, nothing seems to interfere with it, and he drove a ferocious drive straight down the middle of the fairway. The crowd acknowledged the shot generously.

"Maybe nothing too serious after all, given the way he hit that one, Michael?"

"Depressing for us mere mortals to watch, isn't it?

Hold on here, I thought. What's happening? Why hasn't Tuke called over the match referee to report the error? Why hasn't Mickey at least taken the extra club out of his bag? We watched and waited for a further two holes. It was clear that they were not going to report the extra club – no way! Given that Tuke hadn't dropped any shots either, we were beginning to panic and decided to switch on my mobile in order to the contact Mickey's wife. Before we had the opportunity to call, a text message popped up for us.

"If Tuke wins, he will pay into an account of your choice all the winnings for the tournament plus an additional $1million.

Please leave our children alone – PLEASE! Text 'Understand' if you agree to the deal."

It took only a short call to our paymasters to discuss the position. Tuke's lead had lengthened as he maintained his fine form and the immediate challengers struggled themselves. With a press of the index finger the *'understand'* text was on its way. The move was not without risk because not only did Tuke need to win, he had to do so without being caught with the extra club. It was comforting to see Mickey discretely utilise the bag towel again, seeking to cover up the misdemeanour. On balance, the potential returns were worth the risk for us.

Tuke continued to hold his nerve heading towards his first US Masters victory.

As Tuke prepared to collect the prestigious trophy and a cheque for $2,250,000, he was interviewed by the television anchor man, Steffen Kastner.

"Congratulations, Joe, on becoming one of only six men to have won all four majors. How does that feel?"

"Thank you, Steffen. That win was truly priceless."

"Now, I must ask what that phone call was about. We've been inundated with viewer suggestions. Put us out of our misery."

"Steffen, you wouldn't believe me if I told you but let's just say, some things are even more important than golf."